STORAGE   *cop. 2*

FIC   Ashfield, Hel

Regency rogue

995

STORAGE

2 0 (3) note
2

San Diego Public Library

© THE BAKER & TAYLOR CO.

REGENCY ROGUE

The Earl of Dunmorrow and Lady Davina Temple both
want to buy the house of Sir Christmas Dee, following
false rumour that it is for sale. Each is engaged to marry,
but neither is enthusiastic about the proposed nuptials.
Dee invites them to a house-party, but within days he
disappears.

When Davina receives a letter from a friend in Ireland
relating to a murder which had taken place a few months
before, circumstances lead her to believe the earl may be
responsible and, despite the fact that she has fallen in
love with him, her attitude is chilly. He is asked by the
Prince Regent's Secretary to search for Dee and finds
himself in a tangled situation, made worse by the arrival
of his father, a notable eccentric, and also by his growing
love for Davina.

Two escaped convicts, who have taken refuge in the
cellars of Dee's house, are discovered by the earl and
Davina. Each presses them into service in their respective
searches for the truth, which is finally uncovered in an
old, deserted house where danger from an unexpected
source is awaiting them.

By the same author
Beau Barron's Lady

REGENCY ROGUE

**Helen
Ashfield**

Cop. a

St. Martin's Press
New York

First published in Great Britain by Robert Hale Ltd.

Library of Congress Cataloging in Publication Data

Ashfield, Helen.
Regency rogue.

I. Title.
PR6051.S48R4   1982   823′.914   81-23177
ISBN 0-312-66900-3   AACR2

Acknowledgements

I am deeply grateful to the following authors and scholars whose works have furnished me with the facts needed to write this novel:–

The Life and Times of George IV, Alan Palmer.
The Sunny Dome, Donald A. Low.
Brighton, Osbert Sitwell and Margaret Barton.
Wellington: The Years of the Sword, Elizabeth Longford.
Handbook of English Costume in the Nineteenth Century, C. Willett Cunnington and Phillis Cunnington.
The Regency. (Costume), Marion Sichel.
The Age of Illusion: 1750-1848, James Laver.
Costume and Fashion: 1760-1920, Jack Cassin-Scott.
Leisure & Pleasure in the Nineteenth Century, Stella Margetson.

P.B.

One

Anthony St. Romer, Earl of Dunmorrow, was in a good mood. It was a bright spring morning, hardly a cloud in the sky, with birds to sing to him of the joys of summer still to come.

He had earned for himself something of a reputation as a rakehell, being rather too fond of beauties, whom he loved and left without remorse, but no one could deny that he was a remarkably handsome creature. He drove his curricles and phaetons like a devil unleashed, and was equally reckless at the card-tables, but every mother in London worth her salt had tried to snare him for one of her daughters. As for the daughters themselves, they sighed over his tall, graceful figure, dwelling longingly on the fair locks, cut à la Brutus, and the greenish eyes which could be as cold as stone one second and wickedly inviting the next. He had an innate sense of dress, always elegant, even earning the praise of Brummell himself. It was no mean feat, for that gentleman's approval was not easily given.

Yet no one mistook Dunmorrow for an idle dandy. He was a master of the rapier and a crack shot. He had a quick temper and it was accepted by all that to quarrel with the earl would be the act of a suicidal fool.

Now, the unmarried damsels of the *haute monde* were torn between weeping and gnashing of teeth, for, quite unexpectedly, Anthony had offered for the hand of Imelda, daughter of Lord Russell.

He had done so for a number of reasons, none connected

with love. She was eighteen, pretty as a picture, amiable of nature, with a pedigree beyond reproach. Once or twice he had wondered what their life together would be like, but soon dismissed such an irrelevance. It was not at all fashionable to be in love with one's own wife, and passion he could find in any number of beds.

His pleasure that morning was enhanced by the presence of Sir Elliot Dalzell, whom the earl had not seen for two years. Their friendship was not of long standing, but when they had first met at a drum given by Lady Romford they had taken an instant liking to one another, having many things in common. Soon after that, Dalzell had returned to Ireland, where he had an estate and bred fine bloodstock, but a chance meeting at Brook's Club a week before had reunited the men. Now Elliot was riding at the earl's side, on their way to inspect a house which might prove suitable for Dunmorrow's bride.

"I'd forgotten how pleasant Sussex was." Elliot sounded faintly surprised. "It had also slipped my memory how remarkably close you will be to the Regent in his pavilion at Brighton. A most convenient arrangement."

"Quite, and if you will hide yourself away in the bogs, you must expect to have lapses of memory."

Dalzell grinned.

"Perhaps, but Morveley has its compensations. It's a fine sturdy building, with stables second to none."

"Maybe, but one can't stay buried forever in the back of beyond. You should come to London more often."

The earl gave Elliot a side-long glance. No one could call Dalzell an Adonis. His nose was too prominent, his eyes too deep-set, yet he had an air about him which made men look twice, and the female sex reflect upon him a good deal longer. His coat of kerseymere stretched over wide shoulders, the waistcoat concealing a deep barrel chest. His skin was deeply tanned, for he spent most of his time in the open air, when he wasn't dallying with a wench in some peasant's cottage. As he had told the earl, he always favoured women of the lower classes, claiming that they shewed a right and proper gratitude for his attentions.

"I must say I was astounded to hear that you were to marry, Anthony. Never thought after all you said that those witches in town would catch you."

The earl shrugged indifferently.

"Question of carrying on the name, m'dear fellow. One has a duty, and she'll be no trouble. Hope this house will suit; can't waste too much time on such trivial things. Ah, heaven be praised, an inn. We can have food and a bottle of wine to fortify ourselves before we have to attend to this irksome business."

It was past three o'clock before they resumed their journey, the inner man well satisfied, content to ride in comfortable silence.

Anthony thought there was probably no more beautiful sight than the Downs at that time of year, and when they reached the village of Bessingham, just west of Firle Beacon, his opinion was confirmed.

It was small, compact hamlet, with neat flint cottages, and gardens full of flowers and sweet-smelling herbs. There was a church guarding its flock, still shewing traces of its Norman builders, and as they cantered along a winding path they could see a rambling farm to their left, slumberous cows in the fields round about.

When the path widened and began to dip, they had their first sight of Ardley, lying in gardens and parkland which melted into the lower slopes of the Downs themselves. Anthony reined his horse to a halt, his ennui quite gone as he gazed down at the house which had been built when Elizabeth Tudor was on the throne. It wasn't a grand mansion, yet it was large enough for a country seat, and even from that distance its mullioned windows winked like sparkling eyes, luring the beholder on.

Slowly they rode forward again, the earl still silent.

Mature trees stood like sentinels in the background and now the formal flower-beds could be seen, as well as a lily-

pond, statuary, arbours and shrubberies. Beyond these
delights, deer were grazing on the rising ground, smooth
green folds on the bosom of the earth.

"If this were mine," said Dalzell, "I should never part
with it. What did you say the man's name was who lives
here?"

"I haven't mentioned it before, but it is Dee; Sir
Christmas Dee."

"Oh?"

There was a note in Dalzell's voice which made Anthony
turn his head.

"You know him?"

"No."

"I thought perhaps you did. You sounded . . ."

"No, he's not an acquaintance of mine. I was simply
struck by the name, and his folly in parting with a gem like
this."

"Perhaps it's too large for him, or maybe he no longer
has funds to maintain it."

"Then he must be deranged. Nothing would make me
leave here whatever I had to do to raise money to keep it."

"Don't get too attached to it," advised the earl dryly.
"Remember that it is I who intend to buy it."

"But I would outbid you, were it not for my warm feeling
for you, and for the sake of your beloved."

The last comment sat uneasily upon Dunmorrow, for he
had never once thought of Imelda in those terms. He
touched his mount lightly with his whip, urging it on so
that he didn't have to dwell on the point for the time being.

A flunkey admitted them, looking a trifle uncertain,
leaving them in a long, low-ceilinged chamber with open
windows overlooking rose-beds. It was a sparsely furnished
room, yet every piece was so exactly right for its setting that
the earl's heart quickened. Normally an unemotional man,
and not one to worry about the kind of house he occupied,
he felt an instant affinity for the place, curiously anxious to
meet Dee and settle the details of the purchase.

But when Sir Christmas arrived to greet his unexpected guests Anthony was seized with a sharp pang of disappointment. It was not the sight of Dee himself, as sprightly as a boy despite his sixty odd years, but the utter astonishment he expressed upon being asked what figure he placed on the property.

He was rather like a gnome, fluffy white hair just visible under a wig perched crookedly on his head. His face was very lined, as if he had done much living and had enjoyed every moment of it, but the quick smile and friendly dark eyes did nothing to ease the pain of Dunmorrow's dashed hopes.

"Come to buy Ardley, did you say? Well, bless my soul, there's an odd thing. Never entered my head to sell it. Lived here all my life; family before me. Expect I'll die here too."

The earl remained calm, nothing of his frustration permitted to disturb his customary poise.

"I must ask your pardon, Sir Christmas, but I understood that it was your intention to leave Sussex."

"Who told you that?" The wig slipped another inch, Dee clutching at it to prevent a disaster. "Where did you hear such a thing, my lord?"

Anthony hesitated. He really couldn't remember how the information had come to his ears, but it wasn't important. The house which, for some unaccountable reason, he now wanted more than anything in the world wasn't to be his after all.

"I'm afraid I don't know. It must have been no more than idle chatter, and I crave your forgiveness for this trespass, and seeming impertinence."

"No need, no need." Dee waved the apology aside. "Always someone gossiping about this and that, but now you mention the idea ... well ..."

The earl, who had glanced away momentarily to admire a painting above the fireplace, became attentive again. Dee was studying Elliot carefully, his head cocked on one side.

"Think I know you, sir," he said, and nodded

thoughtfully. "Can't place you yet, but the name ..."

Dalzell shook his head.

"We haven't met, for if we had I should have remembered such a felicitous occasion. Perhaps you have purchased a mount or two from my stable at Morveley, and that's why my name seems familiar to you."

Dee was humming to himself.

"Perhaps. Yes, that's probably what it was. Bought a lot of horses in my time." He dismissed the subject, turning back to the earl. "As I was saying, this idea of yours promises to be a good one. Where was I going?"

Dunmorrow was taken aback. Dee seemed wholly unmoved by the intrusion, even interested in what the wagging and uninformed tongues had had to say.

"Scotland, but ..."

"Scotland, eh? Yes, that would be a nice change. Heather, mist, mountains and plenty of good whisky. Think I'd like that. I've probably been here long enough; might be the right thing for me to end my days in the Highlands."

The earl couldn't believe his ears.

"Are you seriously saying that because of this error of mine you are now willing to consider a sale?"

"Why not?" Sir Christmas straightened his toupee again. "Easy to get into a rut, and one must be ready to snatch opportunities when they come. Yes, I'll certainly ponder on it. Meanwhile, why don't you look around, and then we'll have another talk. I must go now. The dogs have to be fed, and they don't like the servants to give them their meat. Arrant snobs, the whole pack of them, but they're affectionate brutes. Go on, go on; take your time. See what you make of it."

Dunmorrow and Elliot watched the door close behind him.

"Can this be some kind of dream, brought about by too much brandy?" enquired the early finally. "No one uproots himself and goes to Scotland, simply because a total stranger suggests the notion to him.''

"No one but Christmas Dee, apparently." Dalzell was drawing off his gloves. "He's an odd one, it can't be denied, but there's no reason why you shouldn't take advantage of the situation."

"It seems wrong somehow."

"Oh come." Dalzell gave a short laugh. "You're not cheating the man. You'll pay a good price, and you didn't force him."

"I know, but ..."

"For pity's sake!" Elliot had no time for his friend's scruples. "Dee himself said one must be ready to snatch opportunities which are offered, and it's obvious that you favour the place. Let's look round in any event; there can't be any harm in that."

Reluctantly, the earl agreed, still feeling a twinge of guilt at disturbing an old man whose wits were fuddled. Yet, as he went from room to room, the sense of belonging there grew deeper, his yearning to own Ardley almost overwhelming. Finally, he succumbed to temptation.

"It's everything I'd hoped for," he said as they made their way back to the room where they had met their host. "There's an air about it which I can't put into words, but is vastly satisfying. You're right, of course. If Dee is still willing, I think I shall make an offer. As you say, I am not coercing him."

"No, certainly you're not, and if you missed such a chance you'd be as crazed as he is. Added to which ..."

Elliot broke off, both men turning as a footman opened the door to admit a girl, dressed in the very height of fashion, followed by an older woman, resplendent in a green silk walking-dress, a monstrous confection of straw and feathers on her head.

For a second no one moved. Then the flunkey said apologetically:

"Forgive me, my lord, but this lady wants to see Sir Christmas too. Come to buy the house, she has; just like you."

* * *

Unlike the Earl of Dunmorrow's day, Lady Davina Temple's had started badly. She had awoken with a headache, due to the lateness of a ball the night before, to find that her maid, Hortensia Moffat, was in one of her militant moods. One always knew when Horty was out of countenance, for she was given to the singing of rousing hymns when put out.

Immediately, Davina and her maid had started to argue about the dress which the former was to wear that day, Horty favouring a white muslin gown with short puffed sleeves and a dainty neck-frill; Davina wanting to wear the saffron sarcenet, which would go so well with her new chip bonnet, trimmed lavishly with ribbons. In the end, the discussion was brought to an abrupt conclusion. Davina had threatened to throw her cup of hot chocolate at her maid, whereupon Horty had stalked out of the room to sulk in private.

Davina had had to attend to her own toilet, for Horty's pets always lasted for two hours at least. She had donned the sarcenet gown, only to discover that it needed a stitch in the hem and that she had to discard it.

Davina, daughter of Gervase Temple, Earl of Hillborough, was nineteen, and ruled her father's house with a rod of iron, chiefly because Hillborough was too lazy to resist and in any event was mere putty in the hands of his only child.

Her hair was reddish-gold, dressed à la Titus, her face an oval of pure ivory. The large hazel eyes could become sharp weapons when she was crossed, her lovely mouth capable of assuming a thin, forbidding line. However, nothing could mar the charm of her small nose and the peerless line of cheek and jaw, whilst her figure caused her father spasms of disquiet when he watched her move with swan-like grace on to the ball-room floor, clad in flimsy finery which left little to the imagination.

Much against the earl's wishes, Davina had chosen for her future husband Sir Peter Guildford, a comely young man of placid disposition, who never argued with her. He had foresworn the evils of strong drink and gambling, turning his attention instead to the writing of poetry, and painting water-colours of mill-streams, meadows, and cows with oddly shaped legs.

Davina had proclaimed herself quite hopelessly in love with Peter, eulogising over his russet-brown hair and soulful eyes. She ignored the fact that he was not over-tall and that his sense of humour was limited to the point of non-existence.

Lately, however, she had been having second, and rather disturbing, thoughts about Guildford. Her pride would not let her voice them aloud, nor permit any other to criticise her chosen spouse. A recent visit to the Marchioness of Bladen, her godmother, had terminated in a brisk exchange of words, when that august lady referred to Peter as a poor ninny in search of a nursemaid.

By mid-morning, Davina had become locked in verbal combat with her father. Hillborough was a bluff, jovial man, who spent most of his time on horseback. Not all of the time, of course, for everyone within twenty miles or so of Hillborough Hall knew of his life-long association with Bessie Lowe, a local farmer's daughter. After the premature death of his wife, Gervase had been lonely, and Bessie was close at hand, and willing. They had produced four sons between them, who, whilst not openly acknowledged by the earl, benefited considerably from his largesse and kindly attention.

Such behaviour had not met with Davina's approval when she learned of it at the age of ten. It was not her father's morals which had concerned her, but the untidy and slipshod way in which he had gone about the liaison. In

her view, her father's mistress should have been kept well
under wraps, and her temper had not improved when the
marchioness, on one of her visits, told her not to be such a
dolt. "Everyone knows, and no one cares," her godmother
had said acidly. "Mind your own business, my girl. You've
too much to say for yourself."

Davina had held her tongue for a while, but Bessie was a
running sore, and when her father had started to talk of
Peter that morning, she was spoiling for a fight.

"I wish you'd think again about this fellow," the earl had
said fretfully. "Wasn't there anyone else you could have
had?"

"Of course there was, but I have chosen Peter, and that is
that."

Hillborough had looked at her broodingly. He knew that
he should never have agreed to the match, for a high-
spirited filly like Davina needed a strong man to keep her in
order, to say nothing of making her happy, but, as usual,
she had had her own way.

"And what's all this about you wanting to buy Christmas
Dee's house? Didn't even know he was selling it."

"Well, you are not apprised of everything, are you? I was
told about it on good authority but you are not likely to be
au fait with current affairs whilst you spend so much time
down at Muckleberry Farm."

She had struck out at her father, meaning to hurt, for she
was miserable herself. Only the previous night she had
flirted outrageously with Lord Croyland, but instead of
calling him out, to shew his love for her, Guildford had
merely observed, with his almost child-like innocence, that
his lordship had been very kind in looking after Davina with
such care.

"And another thing," Davina had continued. "Ardley is
only some fifteen miles away, so that I shall be able to
return often to make sure that everything here is in order."

The earl had groaned inwardly. Much as he worshipped
Davina, her unyielding efficiency and unbending standards

were a great trial to him. For the last year or two, he had
entertained dreams of a dashing knight on a white charger,
who would sweep Davina off her feet and take her to
Northumberland, or some similarly distant parts. Then he
and Bessie could live peaceably and Hillborough Hall could
relapse into the comfortable muddle which it had been
before his daughter had taken it in hand.

He made one last stand.

"You can't go off on your own, and I have to ..."

"Of course I shan't go alone; I'm not a fool. Aunt
Rosamond will accompany me."

"Ah yes, Rosamond."

The earl had felt more gloom wrap itself round him at the
reminder of his unmarried sister, who had come for a short
visit three years ago, and had stayed ever since. Naturally,
she was useful as a chaperon for Davina, but she didn't
approve of Bessie either, and he prayed nightly that she
would soon tire of Sussex, pack her bags and go.

"What does this boy of yours have to say about Ardley?"

Davina had looked mulish.

"I haven't told him yet, and I wish you wouldn't refer to
Peter as a boy. He is twenty years old, and a man."

She had pretended not to hear what the earl had growled
under his breath, and had gone off to find her aunt.

"But I don't want to go to Bessingham." Rosamond had
been petulant. "My dressmaker is coming this afternoon,
you know that."

"She will have to come another day."

"And there is a new book I wish to read."

"You can read it when you return. Really, Aunt, you are
every bit as aggravating as Father."

Rosamond Temple was forty-five, with rich auburn hair,
light-brown eyes and a peaches-and-cream complexion.
Fondness for her food made her curves rather too ample,
but, as she frequently reminded her family, she still
attracted quite noticeable attention from the opposite sex.
She had always maintained that she was a virgin but, when

fixed with Davina's disbelieving eye, was wont to blush and quickly turn the conversation to other matters. She loved Davina dearly, but was somewhat in awe of her and, after another prod or two, had agreed to go with her niece to Bessingham.

It was five o'clock before they reached their destination. Davina was feeling hot, dusty and decidedly not at her best. As they had bowled along in the high-perch phaeton, she had let her thoughts wander back to Peter and his shortcomings, which were becoming more apparent to her with every day that passed. The idea of admitting her choice was a wrong one was not to be entertained, yet, equally, the thought of living with Guildford as his wife made her grow cold inside.

She couldn't imagine now whatever had made her think her feelings for him had been love. He was a gentle, docile creature and she was fond of him, but love!

Even the sight of Ardley didn't comfort her. It was like a jewel lying in a bed of green velvet, but somehow that made things worse. A perfect residence, but a husband who would leave much to be desired.

Yet her spirits were to sink lower still, for, as the flunkey opened the door of a room smelling of roses and beeswax, she found herself confronted by a man who literally took her breath away.

His drab olive coat was cut to perfection, the smallclothes of light biscuit hue immaculate, and the stock could have been arranged by the Beau himself, so cunningly had it been tied. But it wasn't his garb which made Davina feel as if she were suffocating. It was the breadth of shoulder, the long, sinewy legs in skin-tight pantaloons fitted smoothly into shining boots, and a face so handsome that she could scarcely believe her eyes.

For his part, the earl was equally stunned. It had never occurred to him, when carelessly asking for Imelda's hand, that one day he might meet a woman who would make his heart turn over at first sight, and whose mere presence could make his pulse play extraordinary tricks on him. He kept his face under rigid control, yet he couldn't take his eyes off the miraculously coloured hair and a mouth so beautiful that he was seized with an almost irresistible urge to walk over to her and feel the warmth of her lips against his own.

In the end, it was Davina who spoke. She was sharp, because she had to crush without delay the absurd feeling which had crept over her without warning.

"I am Davina Temple," she announced baldly, "and this is my aunt, Lady Rosamond. I'm the Earl of Hillborough's daughter, and I have come to purchase this house."

Anthony and Elliot made their bows. Then the earl straightened up and looked her over from head to toe, a gesture which made delicious colour flood into her cheeks. To prevent himself becoming totally bemused by the sight, he kept his tone as curt as hers.

"And I am Anthony St. Romer."

"Are you indeed?" Her tone was censorious. "The Earl of Dunmorrow, I believe. I have heard about you, my lord."

He raised his quizzing-glass, chilling her with his icy stare.

"Have you? I am flattered. And this, as I was about to tell you when you interrupted me, is Sir Elliot Dalzell."

"Horses," said Davina inconsequentially, trying to avoid the earl's penetrating survey and failing dismally. "I have heard of you too, sir. You breed horses, don't you? My father has purchased some from your stables."

"Yes, I do, and I'm glad to hear I have such a distinguished customer. Lady Rosamond; your servant."

Rosamond inclined her head graciously. She liked a man who looked as if he could be dangerous, and Dalzell shewed every sign of fitting snugly into that category. It was a pity that he and his companion were so young; not near thirty, either of them. Still, some men preferred older women; there was hope yet.

"And what are you doing here?" demanded Davina,

finally breaking the fraught silence which ensued. "Are you a friend of Sir Christmas Dee?"

She knew at once that she shouldn't have asked such a question. It was a bad breach of etiquette, but the harm was already done.

The earl looked bored.

"Whether I am or not, madam, seems to be nothing to do with you, but since your curiosity appears to have overcome your manners, I will put you out of your misery. No, I am not a friend. I have come to purchase Ardley."

"But you can't!" Davina ignored her lapse, and his reprimand, brushing both aside as of no importance. "You cannot do that, for I am here to buy it. It will be my home when I wed."

The earl stiffened imperceptibly. The thought of this impudent hussy's wedding was like the thrust of a knife. She had no right to get married.

"Really? And who is the fortunate man?"

"Sir Peter Guildford, although, to pay you back in your own coin, I cannot see that this is any of your business."

"Guildford? Good God!"

"My lord!"

Elliot's smile deepened, and he was quite disappointed when Dee appeared, scurrying over to them, more gnomish than ever. Another minute or two and Anthony and the ravishing Lady Davina might well have used weapons other than words. The reaction of one to the other was scarcely indifference; the afternoon promised to be a highly entertaining one.

"What a day I am having!" Dee kissed Davina's hand, and then her aunt's. "Dear, dear, two people both wanting my humble abode, and I not even aware that I was going to sell it."

Davina was aghast.

"I don't understand. I was told ..."

Christmas tittered.

"Yes, so was the Earl of Dunmorrow. Funny how these

things get around. As I explained to his lordship, the idea had never entered my mind. Still, I did promise him I'd think about it, and the suggestion of going to Scotland is growing on me."

Davina looked totally bewildered, and in a few brief sentences Anthony laid the situation before her, feeling grim satisfaction at the look of dismay on her face.

Davina saw the look and her lips tightened.

"But you wouldn't sell it to the earl without hearing what I would offer, would you? I am sure, sir, that you would never treat a helpless woman so shabbily."

"Helpless woman?" Dunmorrow raised his glass again, noting the flawless, if inflexible, line of her jaw. "Who is this, if I may be so bold as to ask? I see no such person here."

Davina's eyes were smouldering and it seemed to Anthony that they were like pools of magical fire. However, he was not going to stand any nonsense from her, dismissing such poetic flights of fancy as he addressed Dee.

"I have taken advantage of your kind offer and have inspected the house. It is precisely what I need, and I'm sure that Lady Imelda Russell, my future wife, will be equally content with it."

Davina felt the queerest sensation run through her, utterly deflated by Dunmorrow's last comment. She considered him high-handed, rude and wholly despicable, but the news that he was about to enter into the state of matrimony seemed a far worse blow than finding that she had a rival for Ardley.

She had never met Imelda Russell, but she took a hearty dislike to her there and then. She hadn't met the earl before either, but then she had only recently entered society and for the last month or so had been away on a number of family visits prior to her wedding. She felt rather like an outsider, on the fringe of the polite world, not at all conversant with what was going on, and it made her angrier still.

Dee was shaking his head.

"Dear me; I don't know what to do. I was quite looking forward to the Highlands, but now I think I shall have to stay here, or else offend one or other of you."

There was a tense pause; then Dee's expression lightened.

"Wait! I have a capital suggestion which may be the answer to my predicament. You shall be my guests for a week: you, Lady Davina and Sir Peter; you, my lord, and Lady Imelda." He ignored their baffled expressions, very gallant as he sketched a bow to Rosamond. "You too, of course, dear lady, for your niece must not be exposed to so much adulation as she will surely attract, unless she has a duenna to watch over her. Such a charming one too."

With Lady Rosamond firmly won over to his side, Sir Christmas turned to Elliot.

"Very fond of horses; would like to talk to you about your stables. You'll come too, I hope."

"What is the purpose of this visit?" asked Anthony finally. "You are most gracious, of course, but ..."

"Didn't I explain?"

Dee giggled, whilst the earl and Davina exchanged bleak looks.

"How foolish of me! Why, it is to see whether you like living here at Ardley, blessed as it is with a ghost."

"A ghost!" said Rosamond faintly. "I hadn't realised ... I don't think ..."

"It's hardly ever seen." Dee was reassuring. "You must not let its presence ruin your slumbers. And if you, Lady Davina, or you, my lord, decide you do not care for the place, then I can sell it to the one who does."

It sounded a preposterous plan to Davina, but she knew she had to humour the old man, remaining as calm as she could.

"I am certain already that I shall love the house. It is quite delightful, and I long for it to be mine."

Dee's eyes glinted with amusement.

"Ah, yes, but no doubt the earl feels the same."

His shoulders shook as he glanced from one to the other, as if he fully understood what was going on between his visitors and was highly diverted by it all.

"I don't think, sir, that this is really a practical solution."

The earl took out his snuff-box, using it with such a dextrous twist of the wrist that Davina began to frown again. When Peter tried to use the wretched stuff, he not only covered himself with the aromatic powder, but anyone within five yards of him as well.

"It would be quite wrong to put you to so much trouble. No, it cannot be done."

"Come, Anthony." Elliot was chiding. "Soon I shall have to go back to my Irish bog, as you call it. Nothing would give me greater pleasure than to spend my last few days in England in this most excellent house. Furthermore, I am as anxious to talk to Sir Christmas about the stables as he is. For my sake, if for no other reason, say you accept."

Davina found herself in accord with the earl for the first time since she had met him. She had already decided that Sir Christmas, quaint and kind though he was, was out of his mind. To consider the sale of one's family home, simply because of false rumours, seemed to her to be ridiculous, and not a course likely to be adopted by anyone who was in possession of all his faculties.

Now, as she could see, he was being mischievous, pitting the earl against her and watching the sparks fly. She was about to open her mouth to add her own objections, when Dee said slyly:

"Of course, anyone who did not wish to stay here, even for a short while, could not care enough about Ardley to possess it."

Davina shut her eyes, cursing to herself. It would mean seeing the odious earl every day whilst she was there, but there was no help for it. To refuse would mean Dunmorrow's winning the battle, and that was unthinkable.

The earl had reached exactly the same conclusion, and pressed further by Dalzell, found himself agreeing with the greatest reluctance.

When the details of the visit had been settled, Dee's servants produced tea and then the two parties went on their way.

In the drive, where the horses and carriage waited, Davina chose to ignore the danger signals in Dunmorrow.

"I intend to have Ardley. I'm sorry if you and the woman you are to marry have to look elsewhere, but life is full of such jolts, isn't it?"

"You will find it so, certainly." Anthony looked down at her, torn between a wish to give her a good beating, and a desire to kiss her until the hostility left her dazzling eyes. "I do not choose to look elsewhere. This place will suit me admirably. You and your future spouse must try again. I'm sure that Sir Peter will have many ideas."

"That is the second time you have spoken disparagingly of him." Davina was pale with rage, and something else which she forced firmly into the back of her mind. "You are insulting, my lord, and deserve to be called out for it."

His smile was derisive.

"Then you had better fling down the gauntlet yourself, for Peter Guildford won't, I can assure you."

"You are hateful! I hope I never see you again."

"So do I, for that will mean that you have withdrawn from this bizarre scheme, and I shall be master of Ardley."

"Oh! You are ..."

"Yes, I am," said the earl suavely and made a fine leg. "Until Friday, by which time perhaps you will be in a better temper, and we shall be able to discuss the matter rationally."

"There is nothing to discuss." Davina wanted to cry, a thing she hadn't done since she was five years old. The wretched earl seemed to be undermining her normally resilient spirit, making her feel uncertain and thoroughly out of sorts. "I shall not speak to you when we next meet, and I would ask that you do not address any remarks to me either, for they will not be welcome."

"As you wish." Under his impassive exterior, Anthony was very angry, his longing to box her ears growing stronger by the second. No woman had a right to look as Davina Temple did, particularly as she was about to share her life with Guildford, a harmless but ineffective youth. "That will not be difficult, and I shall be happy to accommodate you. Good-day, madam; Lady Rosamond."

When the earl had mounted up, he said tightly:

"What a farce! A doddering old man who doesn't know what he wants to do, or where he wants to live, and a pert, obnoxious girl who ..."

"She is devastating; you have to admit that."

Elliot was laughing, but Dunmorrow saw nothing remotely humorous in the situation.

"I admit no such thing, and for pity's sake stop talking about her. She has ruined enough of my day as it is. Let's get back to London. If we ride hard, we shall be in time for supper."

"By all means, and I will torment you no more. I'll leave you with your thoughts of Imelda, your own true love."

"Damn you to hell!" shouted the earl, and raced madly down the lane towards the London road as if Satan was snapping at his heels.

Two

"By God, Dunmorrow; can't actually credit it. Sounds like a fairy-tale to me."

"Sir, I swear it is not. Dalzell here will bear me out."

The Prince Regent was in the stables attached to the Pavilion, rumbling with laughter at Dunmorrow's story of a man who was prepared to part with his ancestral home, simply because a stranger asked him to do so. Prinny, his ever-increasing girth stretching his splendid military uniform to the uttermost, paused to look round him.

Damned fine job, the stables. Only completed four years before, and had cost a packet, but well worth it. More like a palace than a place to keep horses; octagonal without, but a perfect circle within, topped by a vast dome which shed light down on the sixty-two stables. The Regent liked to stand in the centre of his new edifice, from which vantage-point he could see into each stall without stirring a foot. Plenty of apartments at high level for the grooms and others working there, with a quite outstanding arch on the south side, opening on to the grounds. Yes, William Porden, the architect, had done well.

"Well, he must be a madman. I wouldn't part with my property so easily, so don't you go trying to talk me into selling you the Pavilion, for you'll get nothing but the rough side of my tongue."

"Sir, I wouldn't dream of depriving you of that which is so near to your heart." Anthony couldn't help smiling. Prinny was like a small boy, gloating over a favourite toy. "How does the work go?"

The Regent heaved a sigh.

"Slowly, I fear, slowly. It's this damned money business, you see. Humphrey Repton's produced some first-class plans for me. Bit tired of chinoiserie, yer know. Thought I'd like a touch of India for a change, but the government's clamped the purse shut. This blasted war with Napoleon's taking every penny, but at least my beauties in here are well-housed."

"Yes indeed."

The earl was watching Elliot's face with amusement. From the first moment that Dalzell had entered the Pavilion, his expression had been one of stupefaction. Prinny was not one for delicate, muted reflections of China, but had filled his villa by the sea with rich, bright colours, furious dragons, and god-like figures of conflict. These, mingled with Moorish and Gothic themes, made the Pavilion look like a theatrical fantasy and, if money was ever forthcoming, it promised to grow more bedazzling, with the spirit of India superimposed on its present glories.

"Know how I got this place, do you?" Prinny gave Elliot an approving nod. Dalzell was obviously greatly impressed and it never occured to the Regent that Elliot's somewhat dazed look was anything but admiration. "Was just a farmhouse once. Came here in '83 because the physicians said the sea-water would aid my swollen glands. Brighthelmstone, they called the village then; more than a village now, eh? Half the world would flock here if it could, what?"

"Yes, sir." Elliot pulled himself together, seeing that the Regent was waiting for more praise. "And how unfortunate they are, these deprived souls who have not had the opportunity of seeing such a sight!"

The irony was quite lost on Prinny, taking Dalzell's words as a well-deserved compliment.

"Well, as I say, I liked Brighton. Sent my Clerk to the Kitchen down here the followin' year to find me somewhere where I could get away from Court. Air's good; Downs first-class for races. Weltje, that was my man, found this. Did all sorts of things for me, did Louis, till he offended me. I altered it a bit at first; later did more. One day, I'll make it a place like no other on earth, just see if I don't. Once this infernal war is over."

"Do we make progress?"

The Regent looked at the earl sombrely.

"Wellington's doing his best: taken Badajoz at last. Damned little jackanapes."

"Wellington?"

"No, blast it, Bonaparte, of course. Got half Europe in his hand, and the Russian Emperor under his thumb. Thank God Nelson washed the French out of the sea. D'yer realise, Anthony, that we've been at war for twenty years. Men getting tired of it: limited travel abroad, and it's played havoc with trade. Can't export a thing unless it's to Portugal or smuggled over."

"Difficult, yet the danger of invasion has gone, surely?"

"Probably; yes, almost certainly. Collingwood's got more ships of the line than the French. Still, we have to keep permanent watch off Antwerp, Brest, Rochefort and Toulon. Never know when that upstart will give the word to sail."

"Such an enemy fleet would be beaten. We are masters of the sea, sir."

"Mm." The Regent was rubbing his chin. "We need to be masters of the land too; in Europe. Difficult to see how it'll all end. Like a see-saw, isn't it? Nelson wins at Trafalgar, and then Boney crushes the Austrians at Austerlitz. No, there's no saying how it'll end. Got to be on our guard too. Another couple of French spies caught in the docks at Portsmouth only last week. Well, that's enough of talk of war. Came here for a few days' peace. Tell me more about this man of yours. Sounds as if he'd made an excellent King's Fool. What's his name?"

"Dee, sir. Sir Christmas Dee."

The Regent, whose attention had drifted off to admire the

sunlight through his fabulous dome, looked quickly at
Anthony.

"Dee?"

"Yes, sir."

The royal eyes were watchful as they switched to Dalzell.
"I see."

"Is there anything wrong?"

The earl was not one of those who subscribed to the belief
that George Augustus Frederick, Prince of Wales, now
Regent of England since his father's latest bout of insanity,
was a fool. Profligate, yes; too fond of wine, women and
gambling, but he had more sense in his head than people
gave him credit for. He had wanted desperately to join in
the fight in Europe, but he was the heir, and his path to
glory was blocked. Instead, he had had to content himself
with the brave uniform of a Colonel of Dragoons, and
remain at home.

Prinny seemed to be lost in thought, but in a trice the
mood had gone as quickly as it had come.

"No, no, nothing wrong. Just an idea which occurred to
me. A slight improvement to the music-room, don't you
know. Well, my boy, let me know whether you or Lady
Davina wins the contest. Sounds a fair piece of fun to me.
Might even ride over and see this place myself. Would spike
both your guns if I bought it, wouldn't it?"

As the earl and Dalzell rode through a square which
looked like honey in the warm light, Elliot said slowly:

"Is he always like that? The Regent, I mean."

"Like what? What are you suggesting?"

Dalzell heard the steel under Dunmorrow's question and
gave a quick laugh.

"Easy, my friend. I'm not suggesting that the prince is
following in his father's footsteps. It was simply that he was
more serious than I had imagined he would be. I always
thought he'd be more interested in the cut of his coat than
the progress of the war. One hears tales, even in the bogs."

The earl relaxed.

"No, Prinny isn't mad; far from it. And I'm glad that you acknowledge it, m'dear Elliot, otherwise I'd have to run you through, and that would be such a waste of energy. Well, to-morrow we're for Bessingham, and that tedious woman." His lips were tight. "I swear I shall stand no nonsense from her this time. Ardley is going to be mine, and if I have to put that vixen in her place to get it, so be it."

Elliot hid his smile as they reached the Old Ship Tavern, where they were to pass the night. Perhaps Christmas Dee's phantom wouldn't appear to afford him entertainment, but the struggle between Lady Davina and Anthony would make an excellent substitute. Indeed, the passage of arms between two fiery creatures of flesh and blood, whose attraction to one another was obvious to everyone but them, would be a great deal more amusing than Dee's elusive wraith. Yes, as the Regent had said, it would be a fair piece of fun.

* * *

At three o'clock on Friday morning two shadowy figures stumbled through the darkness, spent and weary, as finally they found themselves beside the outbuildings lying behind Ardley.

The first man, Horace Codder, had a squarish, unshaven face, with small watery eyes and the very minimum of flesh on his bones. Despite this, he was a hard man who had led a hard life, and many had underestimated the strength of his gangling frame. His fellow-traveller, Mortimer Smythe, was a complete contrast to Codder, being short, plump and highly nervous, his face pasty as he kept close to his companion.

The only thing which the two had in common was the fact that the day before they had escaped from Stockland Gaol, just outside Selmeston. It was not simply the atrocious conditions in the prison which had driven them to such a course, nor the sadistic nature of the gaoler. It was the fact that they had been sentenced to transportation, and, as Codder had said, anything was worth chancing to avoid such a fate.

"What's this place do you reckon, Horace?" Smythe was cold, and very hungry. He wasn't really sure that the penal colony would have been much worse than his present situation, but he was a born follower. "Think it's a shepherd's hut, do you?"

"'Ow would I know?" Codder was cold too, and needed food as much as Mortimer, but he was tough enough to withstand these twin miseries without mewing like a kitten. He was beginning to think that Smythe was going to be a liability, but if that proved to be the case there was an easy solution to the problem. "If it is, and there be anyone inside, I'll soon 'ave their guts."

Smythe saw the knife in Horace's hand and yelped.

"No, no! Not that, for Jesus' sake! D'yer want to swing?"

"Rather dangle at a rope's end than git aboard that hell-ship." He pushed Smythe out of his way. "If yer can't stand the sight o' blood, be on yer way, and keep yer voice down, or I'll do you first."

Petrified, Mortimer followed Codder into the brick-built haven. It was empty and Codder grunted in satisfaction.

"Good. This'll do until the mornin'. Git a bit o' rest 'ere, then we'll be on our way."

"I'm starving. What about a bite to eat?"

"Oh yes, yer lordship, and what'll yer 'ave? Roast beef and chicken pie, and maybe a bit o' pork? Shut up, yer stupid runt. Yer belly'll stay empty till we're out o' this place."

Mortimer dared say no more, crouching down against the hard wall, trying not to listen to the plaintive rumbling of his stomach. Their exhaustion was such that both men were soon snoring, and might indeed have slept well into the middle of the next day had not a deafening cry from an active chanticleer woken the pair of them.

"Gawd, what's that?" Mortimer struggled to his feet,

staggering towards Codder who was easing the door open. "Horace, what was it?"

"A cock, yer playguy fool; what d'yer think it was? Christ!"

He leapt back, closing the door rapidly.

"Horace! What is it? What's wrong?"

Codder looked down at the sweaty face of his travelling companion.

"This ain't no shepherd's hut. There's a bloody great 'ouse out there, and people too. Servants and stable-boys and the like."

Mortimer whimpered, earning a cuff from Codder.

"Shut up, yer clod, that won't 'elp. We've got ter git out of 'ere without bein' seen, though Gawd knows 'ow. 'Ere, wait a minute though. What's that over there? Trap-door, ain't it?"

They hurried over to the far side of the barn, hesitating for a second.

"Well, we're done fer anyway." Codder was philosophical. "Might as well try it."

To their relief, there was a flight of steps leading down into darkness, and carefully they lowered themselves, closing the trap behind them. After a short walk, the passage they were in turned sharply right and Codder jumped back again.

"Wait ... careful. We're under the 'ouse, that's where we are. Some light along there; them's the kitchens, fer sure."

Mortimer's teeth were chattering.

"Horace, what we goin' ter do?"

"Keep yer bone-box fastened. D'yer want everyone to 'ear yer? Come back 'ere; the way we came in. Thought I saw a cranny we might 'ide in."

Gingerly Codder pushed the door open, Mortimer wincing as it creaked through lack of use.

"'Ere, this'll do us fine. No one uses this, that's certain; even a candle left for us. What d'yer say to that?"

"We can't stay 'ere. They'll find us."

"Not fer a while. Like I says; ain't used." Codder had lit the candle and was examining his new home. "We'll be all right 'ere. Wait till nightfall, then we'll be on our way, or maybe we won't."

"Eh?"

Codder grinned evilly at Mortimer's fear.

"Well, it's dry in 'ere; roof over our 'eads. Later on, when it's quiet, I'll slip off and git some food. Let the guards tire themselves out lookin' fer us fer a day or two. Then we'll move on."

"I don't likes it."

"Not asked ter, are yer? Sit down, or I'll lay yer down, permanent like."

"Yes, Horace."

Meekly, Smythe crept into a dirty recess, hugging his knees up to his chin. It was all far worse than he had imagined it would be, and the prospect of transportation seemed almost welcome at that moment.

"'Ope it'll be quiet soon. Fair famished, I am."

Codder gave him a sharp kick.

"It'll be soon enough. Now, 'old yer tongue; I wants ter think."

* * *

Davina and her aunt, escorted by Sir Peter Guildford, arrived at about eleven-thirty on Friday morning.

Bearing in mind that she would soon be seeing the objectionable earl again, Davina had taken particular care with her toilet and was wearing a dainty dress of light green muslin, trimmed with ribbon, under a silk pelisse, her face framed by a most fetching bonnet.

There hadn't been room in the phaeton for all the luggage which she and Rosamond wished to bring with them, and so Horty had been instructed to finish packing and follow on in a couple of days.

Sir Christmas welcomed them in delight, complimenting

the two ladies on their appearance, taking stock of Guildford as they exchanged a courteous word or two.

"Now, before you are taken to your rooms," said Dee, "you must meet my other visitors. I forgot to tell you before, but Lord Stuart Barminster, his wife, Jessica, and their friend, Sir Peter Whittingham, are also to be with us for a few days. Ah, my dears, now let us see about introductions.

Davina wasn't sure that she cared for the thought of other house guests. Somehow they seemed to get in the way of the main issue, and another matter which she still refused to consider for a second.

Stuart Barminster was stout, with a ruddy face and hot blue eyes. He held Davina's hand a shade too long, and she felt like reaching into her reticule for a handkerchief to wipe her glove clean. His wife was tall, blonde and very thin in spotted cambric. She gave Davina and Rosamond a blank look, as if she thought them beneath her notice. Then her almond-shaped eyes slid back to the good-looking Sir Percy, quite ten years her junior.

Davina kept her sweetest smile for Whittingham, triumphant when he went as red as a turkey-cock, and Lady Jessica's glare made her face more unprepossessing than ever.

After that, Davina and her aunt went to repair the damages of travelling.

Rosamond sank down in a chair, very much put out.

"Well, I do declare that this is most irregular. I cannot imagine what Sir Christmas is thinking of."

Davina was considering the question of whether a touch of rouge would make her eyes brighter, deciding that it really wasn't necessary. She would be able to deal with Dunmorrow quite satisfactorily without such artificial aids.

"Mm?" She was attending to her hair, hardly listening to her aunt. "What did you say?"

"Do pay attention! I said I thought it mightily improper that Sir Christmas should invite you here at a time when that Barminster woman and Sir Percy are with him."

"But why? They look harmless enough, although I agree that Lady Jessica is not a very pleasant person. Do you think I should change my gown? Is this one grubby?"

"Never mind your gown, and as to why you shouldn't be here, Jessica Barminster and Sir Percy are lovers. Everyone knows that; they make no secret of it."

"I didn't know."

Davina was neither shocked nor interested. Very few kept their love-affairs to themselves, and her mind was dwelling on the manner in which she should greet the earl. Cold and distant, or charmingly, leaving the *coup de grâce* for later.

"Well, no, of course you didn't, but you haven't been in society long enough to know about such things. I can't understand Stuart. He must be as blind as a bat not to see what is going on under his nose."

"Perhaps he sees, and doesn't care. For goodness sake, don't fuss. What does it matter?"

"It matters a good deal. Loose women should not be allowed to ..."

Davina turned from the mirror.

"You are not going to tell me yet again how you have clung to your innocence, Rosamond, are you, for I must tell you frankly, before you begin, that I suspect you have done far worse things in your day than Lady Jessica is capable of."

"Really!"

Rosamond was only half-annoyed. It wasn't entirely displeasing for the lovely young Davina to realise that her aunt had also had her day.

When a maid arrived to see if they required assistance, she was very agitated, white as bleached linen. Davina and Rosamond, both extremely kind at heart, expressed immediate concern.

"Good gracious, girl," said Lady Rosamond. "Whatever is wrong with you? Are you faint? Davina, there's a brandy-flask in my jewel-box; give it to me please."

"No, no, m'lady, I mustn't." The girl was plump, with

eyes like saucers. "Mr Rourke, the butler, is ever so strict. I'd be thrown out if 'e found I'd touched a drop of liquor. 'Sides, I'm not faint. It's the ghost."

"What!" Rosamond let out a shriek and sat down again. "Surely you're mistaken."

Davina frowned slightly. She remembered that Dee had mentioned a phantom, but she had assumed he was jesting. Now, it seemed, it was not so."

"You saw it?"

"Not me, miss; it were Mary. Downstairs, near the kitchen. Ever so tall, she said, and thin like a skeleton. She had hysterics on the spot, but though some of the men went along the passage to look, there weren't nothin' there."

"No, of course there wasn't." Rosamond took out her fan and waved it briskly to and fro. "Lot of superstitious nonsense. There are no such things as ghosts."

"Well, if you says so, m'lady, but I wouldn't go down into them cellars after dark if I was you."

"I am not likely to." Rosamond was haughty. "Whatever next?"

"Sorry, m'lady." The maid was near to tears. "I didn't mean ..."

"No, of course you didn't." Davina was soothing. "What is your name?"

"Alice, miss."

"Well, Alice, here's half a sovereign. You and Mary buy yourselves something nice next time you go to the fair. I expect you have a fair here, don't you?"

Miraculously, Alice's terror had melted away as she stared at the coin in delight.

"Oh, yes, we do! Every Michaelmas; it's lovely."

"I'm sure it is. Now off you go; we can manage."

"I'm not at all certain that this whole visit is not a great mistake." The fan moved more vigorously than ever. "First, Jessica Barminster, and now a spectre."

"There aren't such things; you've just said so. Now do get ready. It's almost time for luncheon."

"Do you think the earl and his party are here yet?"

"I have no idea." Davina was studiedly off-hand. "He is of no interest to me whatsoever."

Rosamond glanced at her niece's reflection in the looking-glass. Hillborough's sister was no blue-stocking, but she had a great deal of common sense and had lived long enough in the world to recognise that particular note in a person's voice.

"Heavens above!" Rosamond laid her scent-bottle down. "Not another complication, surely."

"I have no idea what you mean." Davina didn't look at her. "And there's the gong. Don't dawdle, Aunt; it would be ill-mannered to be late."

She went downstairs, leaving Rosamond still shaking her head, to follow.

The light repast was not graced by the presence of the earl, and Davina felt a pang of disappointment. Perhaps he had decided not to come after all. She told herself roundly that this would be a most excellent thing, since she would then have no rival for Ardley. Excellent or not, it took her appetite away, and she only toyed with her food as Lord Stuart began to fulminate on the ills from which England was suffering at that moment.

"Don't know what'll become of us all," he said moodily, stuffing his mouth full of cold chicken. "Men have wrecked the machines in two of my mills in Lancashire. They say the damned things are stealing their livelihood from them. Utter nonsense, of course, though this infernal war is destroying trade. No markets, d'yer see? Food's scarce, and bread's such a price that the poor can't afford to buy it. They always get restive when that happens. And look at the businesses which have closed down. I tell you, it's getting serious. Wish Wellington would finish off that wretched Corsican, and then things would pick up again."

"Do be quiet, Stuart." Lady Jessica was impatient. "We don't want a lecture from you about the war, or bankrupt firms. Go and tell the government if you feel so strongly about these things." Her tone changed to silky softness. "Sir Percy, would you be good enough to pass me the salt?"

It was four o'clock before the earl and his friends arrived. He and Dalzell occupied one phaeton, the vehicle groaning under the weight of boxes and trunks. The second carriage brought Lady Imelda, her maid and a much more modest amount of luggage.

"One might think he intended to stay for a month at the very least," observed Davina tartly, quite overlooking the fact that she and her aunt had a whole curricle of trunks on their way. "What a conceited creature he must be!"

"Perhaps some belong to Lady Imelda." Rosamond wasn't so critical. She liked a man to be well-turned out and found no fault in the earl for bringing what was necessary to maintain his appearance. "I expect they are."

"I don't. I'm sure they are all his. Popinjay!"

But as she watched him she found to her chagrin that she was almost trembling. He was so very handsome and tall. The dark-blue superfine coat couldn't have been improved upon; the stock was perfect, as before. There wasn't a single crease marring the light-coloured breeches, despite his journey, not a speck of dust spoiling the shine of his hussars.

She wished she hadn't been so vehement in her demand that he should not speak to her when they next met. The thought that he might oblige, made her feel quite hollow inside.

Peter looked immature and unsure of himself next to the earl and Davina's irritation grew. Dunmorrow really was the most maddening man she had ever had the misfortune to meet.

She had painted so detailed a portrait in her mind of Imelda Russell that the sight of the small girl who curtsied shyly to her shattered another illusion. Imelda wasn't at all the *grande dame* Davina had imagined, but was young and diffident, with dark silky curls, skin like cream and huge brown eyes.

She looked as though she expected a rebuff, and Davina found herself greeting her warmly, quite forgetting to hate her for the moment. When the earl introduced Imelda, he was so disinterested that it seemed as though the girl was about to burst into tears.

Davina was on the point of taking Dunmorrow to task for his unkindness, when she saw an expression on Peter's face she hadn't seen before, and grew very still. It was a kind of joyous disbelief, mingled with admiration, and his obvious pleasure was reflected in the girl who blushingly surrendered her hand for Guildford's salute.

Peter had never looked at Davina in that way, but then she had to admit she hadn't gazed at him in wonder as Imelda was doing now. A week ago, Davina wouldn't have realised what was happening, but she knew now, sick at heart because fate had dealt the cards so badly.

When Dunmorrow came up to her, he had either forgotten what she had said, or decided to ignore it, for he made a leg, kissing her finger-tips with such an air that the uncertainty in her turned to actual alarm.

"Your servant, madam. And are you enjoying yourself?"

"I have only been here an hour or two."

"Yes, of course."

She thought the comprehensive glance which he gave her must have taken in the very stitching of her gown, and wished she had taken time to change into the yellow silk with the flounces at the hem.

"Never mind." He ignored her discomfiture. "When this place is mine, you and Sir Peter must come for a much longer stay."

She shook herself out of her day-dream. He was deliberately goading her and she was determined not to give him the satisfaction of seeing her lose her temper.

"Do you know," she replied in honeyed tone, "that is exactly what I was going to say to you. You and Lady Imelda will be most welcome at any time, when I am mistress of Ardley."

He gave a suspicion of a smile, acknowledging the flick of her verbal rapier.

"You are too kind." Somehow, he had contrived to lead her away from the others, out of earshot. "And talking of mistresses, what on earth is old Dee up to? I didn't expect to find Generous Jessie here."

She only just managed to smother a laugh in time.

"Is that what you call her?"

"It's what all London calls her, and with good reason." He took out his jewelled quizzing-glass, turning to scrutinize the unfortunate lady, deep in conversation with Sir Percy. "Whittingham must be mad, or in need of money."

"You are scarcely gallant. Lady Jessica is very pretty."

The glass was slipped back into his pocket, his attention on Davina again.

"She's not in the least pretty. For heaven's sake don't start mouthing polite lies. Your blunt, if somewhat offensive, manner of telling the truth is the most attractive thing about you."

The colour washed into her cheeks and the sight was so breathtaking that the earl nearly leaned forward and kissed one of them.

"You are not only lacking in gallantry." Davina couldn't imagine why she felt like crying every time she spoke to the earl. "You are monstrously uncivil too. Be good enough to leave me."

"If you insist, but I had hoped you would walk round the gardens with me, and tell me how I should alter them, after I have taken possession."

That was too much for Davina, and her good resolutions flew out of the window.

"You are unbearable! I detest you!"

He smiled again, this time in rather a different way.

"That's a very good sign. It's close to another emotion, so they say."

"I don't know what you're talking about." She could feel

tears behind her eyes, praying that he would leave her, and quickly. To make a spectacle of herself in front of this arrogant nobleman would destroy her. She would never be able to hold up her head in society again. "Will you please go!"

"Very well, for now, but think about what I have said."

He sauntered off, and she reached hastily for her handkerchief, assuring herself firmly that she had a small speck of dust in her eye which had to be removed.

But it wasn't until she rejoined Rosamond and the others that she regained her senses sufficiently to realise what Dunmorrow had meant.

'Love is very close to hate.'

Her cheecks became warm again, this time with pure anger.

"Damn you for that, my lord," she said to herself. "Now I will most certainly have Ardley, no matter what I have to do to get it."

Three

Three days passed without incident. Christmas was a genial host, his cook most competent, and the countryside was ideal for walks and rides. It seemed to Davina that Peter and Imelda spent more and more time together, yet she made no move to remind Guildford where his place should be. She didn't want him, and that was the truth of it. She knew only too well whom she did want, and spent many hours castigating herself because of it.

On the fourth morning two pieces of information were imparted to Dee's startled guests as they arrived in the dining-room to partake of breakfast.

The first was of small significance, being another whisper which ran round the table that a second serving-girl had seen a long, very thin shadow in the basement.

It had occurred already to Davina that there had been a change in the manner of Dee's staff since yesterday morning. They had become nervous, shifty and anxious to get back to their own quarters as soon as any particular duty had been performed. She hadn't thought much of it, putting it down to the fact that Mary thought she'd seen a ghost, and Lady Jessica was about to put an end to that foolishness.

"These stupid wenches," she said tartly, "it's just hysteria. One of them sees a corner of a cupboard or some such thing, and imagines the place is haunted, and now the whole lot of them believe it too. Even the men seem affected. Why, one of the footmen was quite insulting yesterday afternoon, and bolted off whilst I was in the middle of asking for some wine. And where is Sir Christmas this morning?''

Davina looked across at Dunmorrow, but it appeared he wasn't listening. Neither Lady Jessica nor unquiet souls seemed to bother him, but when a flunkey came in, his face almost grey, and bent to whisper in the earl's ear, the latter's eyes narrowed.

"Are you certain? Perhaps he has gone riding."

"What is it?" demanded Lady Jessica. "Really! Whispering in that rude fashion!"

Davina felt a sense of apprehension, glancing round the table at the others. Peter and Imelda were looking into each other's eyes, oblivious to what was going on. Rosamond was enjoying her meal; Stuart Barminster was still grumbling about the Regent and his policies, Sir Percy lending him half an ear.

At last Barminster realised that something was afoot, laying down his knife.

"Yes, speak up, man. If you've got something to say, let's all hear it. What's wrong with you?"

The servant shrank back, but Davina got the impression that it wasn't only Barminster's bark which caused him to cringe. He just shook his head, and it was the earl who said shortly:

"It seems that our host has disappeared. His bed wasn't slept in, and he's nowhere to be seen."

There was a chorus of concern, quickly stilled by Dunmorrow's raised hand.

"Has anything like this ever happened before?" He was considering the servant thoughtfully. The man was near to fainting; it was most odd. "Has Sir Christmas ever gone away before, without warning?"

"Well, m'lord, as a matter of fact he has." The servant kept his eyes down. "Often goes off, and none of us know what happens to him. Comes back again, of course."

"Well then ..." Dunmorrow was still puzzled. There was

more to all this than met the eye. "If that is so, why are you so ...?"

"Are you saying," interrupted Lady Jessica in high indignation, "that Sir Christmas has invited us to stay with him, and then simply gone off and left us, without a word?"

"It would seem so." Dunmorrow dismissed the flunkey with a wave of his hand. "Very well, but you'd better look round the grounds to make sure. See if one of the horses is missing, but, from what you say, there seems no cause for alarm."

The man gave a jerky bow and almost ran from the room.

"It's quite outrageous." Barminster went back to his plate of cold roast beef. "Never heard the like of it. Man must be deranged or damnably rude. Didn't want to come in the first place."

"Do hold your tongue, Stuart."

Whilst Jessica was dealing with her husband, Elliot said softly:

"Do you think there's anything seriously wrong, Anthony? Even if Dee does wander off now and then, surely he wouldn't do so when he has guests."

"Perhaps not, yet he's by no means a conventional character. He may simply have forgotten that we were here. I've known other men, at least, one other man, who is quite capable of doing the same thing."

His tone was somewhat bitter, but when he didn't respond to Elliot's interrogative eyebrow the latter said:

"That man was paralysed with fear. Why should he be, if this has happened before? He's not the only one either. Since yesterday lunch-time the whole of Dee's staff appear to be in mortal dread. Had you noticed?"

"I could hardly fail to do so. I'm beginning to believe ..."

He did not have time to finish the sentence, for another minion had come in, shaking like one with the palsy, and with even worse news.

"Fallen down the stairs?"

Rosamond and Jessica gave startled cries and, under the

cover of the damask cloth, Peter reached for Imelda's hand, squeezing it to comfort and reassure her.

"Yes, m'lord. It's Gunn, one of the footmen. Lying at the bottom of some steps in the basement, dead as mutton."

Rosamond gave a high-pitched scream and Davina gripped her arm.

"Do be quiet, Aunt. It isn't you who is lying there, so you've no cause to create such a scene. Well, my lord, since the servants seem to be turning to you for help and advice, what do you propose to do?"

Dunmorrow rose gracefully, touching his lips with his napkin.

"I propose to go and look at the late lamented Gunn," he said mildly, "although what use that will be, I really don't know. Is there a doctor living nearby?"

The flunkey shook his head, and the earl noticed the unsteadiness of the man's hands, pensive again. Well, perhaps the sight of one of his fellows lying dead in the basement could explain it.

"Ten miles or more away, and laid up with gout, so we've been told."

The earl sighed.

"How excessively inconvenient! Are you coming, Elliot?"

"I shall come too." Davina stood up, brushing Rosamond's protests aside. "Do stop it, Aunt. The responsibility for dealing with this matter rests no more upon the earl than upon me. After all, it is I who intend to purchase Ardley from Sir Christmas."

"Really?" Sir Percy looked surprised. "Never knew that."

"Why should you, sir?"

Peter half-rose. He knew he had neglected Davina disgracefully since Imelda's arrival. At first, he had been perfectly content with the prospect of marrying so competent, decisive and wealthy a girl as Davina, but lately he had been chafing a mite. She was beautiful, of course, and highly intelligent, but she treated him as if he were about four years old. He had not been at all sure, during the last few weeks, whether the match was going to be a success, and as soon as he had met Imelda he had known beyond doubt that it wouldn't be.

Imelda was fragile and sweet and gentle. He made him feel protective and important for the first time in his life, and he was already quite hopelessly in love with her.

"Sit down, Peter." Davina was firm. "You will be of no help at all. Stay here, and look after Rosamond and Imelda."

For a second he was rebellious. Slapped like a naughty infant and reminded yet again how useless he was. Then he looked down at Imelda.

"Yes, please do stay." She was imploring. "I shan't feel safe at all if you leave me."

The earl was almost sorry for Guildford, but the latter had no one to blame but himself. He should have taken his riding-crop to Davina Temple a long time ago.

"One moment," he said, fixing Davina with a cool stare. "If you are prone to the vapours, I beg you to stay here too. I'm sure Sir Peter can manage to comfort you, as well as the other ladies, and I don't want to deal with two bodies at the same time."

Davina's temper rose at once. If his lordship imagined he could put her in her place that easily, he must be disillusioned as fast as possible.

"I am not in the habit of fainting, and I intend to come with you."

"Very well, but don't say you were not warned."

At the foot of some steps at the far end of the basement, they surveyed the remains of Robert Gunn. Davina hadn't expected the man to be lying in such a crooked position, nor to find open eyes staring blindly at her. His skin was drained of blood, so white that, even from where she stood, she knew it would be as cold as stone if touched.

The earl, who seemed to miss nothing, said quickly:

"Go upstairs. You can do nothing here."

"No ... no. I'm quite all right. It's just that he looks so ..."

"... dead? Yes he is; very dead." Anthony rose from his inspection of the body. "When was he found?"

The cluster of servants grew closer, their faces pinched and full of something the earl didn't like. They would have seen corpses before; why were they so terrified?

"Just now." It was Rourke who answered, tugging at the stock round his thick neck. "It was Biddy, here, who stumbled over him in the dark."

"Just now? But surely you've all been up for hours? Why wasn't he discovered before? He's been dead for some time by the look of him."

"Well, m'lord, we don't use them steps much. Fact is, we hardly ever go along that far; that's why there were no lights. Nothing much up that end, 'cept two or three storerooms round that corner."

"Then why was Biddy there? Which of you is Biddy?"

A shrinking girl of twenty or so, drowned in a large mob-cap and voluminous apron, was pushed forward, but she was crying so hard that Dunmorrow could get no sense out of her. He had to be content with Rourke's explanation that the maid had heard a noise and had gone to investigate. It was patently untrue. Biddy was far too scared to investigate anything.

Accepting the falsehood for the moment, Dunmorrow's attention returned to the body. He didn't like the way the dead man was lying; in fact, there were many things he didn't like about the whole situation, including the fact that Dee was missing.

"I see. Well, there's nothing to be done for him, poor fellow. Move him into one of the stores, and I'll see about the arrangements which have to be made."

"Are you sure it was an acc....."

Dunmorrow's scowl warned Davina silently not to go on, but she had to ask.

"Are you certain that it was an accident?"

The staff drew back, the women completely overcome by such a suggestion, the men equally horror-struck.

"Yes," replied the earl blandly, "of course it was. What else could it have been?" He snapped his fingers. "Move him, as I've told you, and then get on with your work. Let me know when the grounds have been searched. Lady Davina, will you please go upstairs, or do I have to carry you?"

Davina turned and fled. Dalzell watched the corpse being moved. Then he said quietly:

"That wasn't an accident."

"I know." Anthony kept his voice down. "But for God's sake don't let anyone hear you say so. The whole thing is trying enough as it is. I'll give Dee an hour or so to return, and then I'll ride over to Alciston. Should be a physician there."

"A Bow Street runner would be more appropriate."

"Quite, but we are unlikely to find one in a Sussex village. However, there's probably a parish constable, or some such official. Damned awkward – all of it. And where on earth has Dee got to?"

"Where indeed? And if the good Robert didn't fall downstairs by mischance, who pushed him?"

Anthony met Dalzell's quizzical gaze.

"That is what we shall have to find out, but for the moment no one must be told of our doubts. It was an accident; nothing more. We shall have a riot on our hands if they suspect anything else."

"I shan't say a word." Elliot's smile was not amused. "But you do realise, don't you, that someone in this house already knows the truth. One of us here at Ardley has just committed murder."

*   *   *

Hortensia Moffat arrived at ten o'clock, grumpy and tired.

"Funny lot of servants in this place," she said, dumping a large box on the floor. "Seem to be frightened of their own shadows. I would have been here two days ago, but when I tell you of the mishaps I've had ..."

"Please don't," said Davina hastily. She was beginning to get over the sight of Gunn's body, her mind turning instead to the question of whether the earl would really have carried her upstairs had she not gone when she did. "Horty, we've got enough trouble here, without listening to your disasters."

"Trouble?" Hortensia was agog, for she thrived on adversities, and she gave Davina and Lady Rosamond a closer look. "What sort of trouble? You look quite peaky, m'lady. Aren't you well?"

Rosamond was drinking a glass of brandy, trying not to let her teeth chatter. Davina had been as white as a sheet when she had come back from the cellar, and there was still no sign of Sir Christmas. A horrid uncertainty had lodged itself in Rosamond's mind, and it wouldn't go away.

"Yes, I'm well enough, but first Sir Christmas has disappeared, and then a servant fell down a flight of steps and killed himself. Horty, we should never have come here. I knew it was a mistake. The whole plan was bedevilled from the start."

"What did I tell you?" Hortensia was full of self-satisfaction. "Didn't I say it was a stupid idea? But Lady Davina wouldn't listen, would she? Oh no, her ladyship wouldn't ..."

"Stop it!" Davina was remembering Gunn's empty eyes, envying Imelda because she had someone to comfort her. Of course, Peter wouldn't have been any use to her, Davina, even if he had recalled that they were engaged. Rosamond and Horty weren't what she wanted either. "What is that? Is it a letter for me?"

"Yes, it came just after you'd gone. Now, if you ask me ..."

"I don't. Just get on with the unpacking, and let me read this. Oh, do go on with you!"

"Very well, if my opinion isn't wanted."

Horty slammed a trunk open and began to shake the delicate gowns free of creases, singing very loudly as she did so. Plaintively, Rosamond begged her to stop, taking another sip of brandy, but Davina was by now totally unaware of either of them.

The epistle was from Mirabel Southey, who lived in Ireland with an aged aunt. Davina and Mirabel had been friends since the age of five, and corresponded every so often, more as a matter of habit than anything else.

The first few paragraphs were full of bits of gossip, but then Davina felt the colour fading from her face again.

"My dear," Mirabel had written. "It is so long since I put pen to paper that I have not yet told you of the scandal we had here a few months ago, just before the end of last year. It was all quite shocking, I can tell you, and concerned an Englishman. They say he killed a man in cold blood, but because he was the son of a marquis, or some such nobleman, he was not brought to book, but escaped justice entirely, and left the country. My aunt was very moved by the death of the local man, for he was married, with so many children that everyone had lost count of them. Aunt Mabel felt the murderer should be made to pay for his terrible deed, and so she wrote to an old friend of hers who lives in Sussex, Sir Christmas Dee – what an odd name to be sure. Aunt thought, despite the fact that he was growing old, and inclined to be somewhat erratic, he might be able to help. For my part, I doubt it, and whether or not Sir Christmas has taken any steps to find the culprit, I have no idea. I expect that he's forgotten all about it. I wish I knew who the Englishman was, but my aunt wouldn't tell me. She said it was better that I didn't know. Now to other things ..."

Davina's hand fell to her side, the rest of what Mirabel

had written ignored. In normal circumstances, she would have paid scant heed to what her friend had written, but this was too much of a coincidence. Mirabel's aunt had sent a letter to Dee about a young Englishman who had committed murder, and now Sir Christmas had disappeared and one of his servants had died.

She felt a fresh quiver run through her. Dunmorrow said it had been an accident, but was it? He had soon sent the servants packing and had ordered her upstairs, almost as if he didn't want anyone to examine the body too closely. Not that she could have brought herself to draw nearer to that waxen face, but still ...

She shook herself mentally. She was being too silly for words. Just because Mirabel's aunt happened to know Dee, it didn't mean that ... She closed that avenue of thought abruptly and went to help Horty, whose temper had improved remarkably, due to half a cup of brandy from Lady Rosamond's secret store. When Davina had finished putting the last glove away, she knew she couldn't postpone what she had to do any longer, and went in search of Dunmorrow.

"Has Sir Christmas been found?"

He turned to look at her and what she felt was worse than any physical pain. Anthony and Imelda? She wouldn't let herself dwell on such a dreadful prospect.

"Apparently not." He thought she looked rather drawn, wishing that he could pull her into his arms and tell her not to worry; that he was there to take care of her. "I shall be leaving in about an hour to get help."

"Yes." She wasn't quite sure how to go on, but it had to be done. "My lord, this may seen an odd question to put to you at such a time, but have you ever been to Ireland?"

"Yes, many times. Why do you ask?"

His green eyes were on hers and she felt her mouth dry.

"Simply that I have had a letter from a friend of mine who lives in Omagh. Were you there recently?"

"In Ireland? Yes, at the end of last year."

He seemed to her watchful, and she said lightly:

"I expect you went to see Sir Elliot."

"As a matter of fact, I didn't. There wasn't time."

She murmured an excuse and left him, and his frown returned. Why should Davina Temple suddenly start asking him questions about visits to Ireland? The fact that she had an acquaintance living in Omagh seemed an inadequate reason, yet it was obvious that his answer had been important to her. He decided he would take the matter up with her when he had a moment to spare; meanwhile, he had more pressing things on his mind.

In the garden, hidden away where no one could see her, Davina was trying to keep calm. Of all the people now at Ardley, Anthony St. Romer seemed to her the most capable of murder, if murder there had been. But why should he bother to kill a flunkey?

The sunshine was warm, but Davina could feel goose-pimples on her arms. The answer was really quite easy. If Robert Gunn had seen something he shouldn't have done, such as the slaying of Christmas Dee, he would have had to be silenced. There was a lump in Davina's throat, and she found it was hard to swallow. Why should Anthony want to see Dee dead?

Mirabel's letter had furnished the answer to that. If the earl was the Englishman who had killed the man in Ireland, Dee would have been told about it by Mirabel's aunt, for the latter knew the killer's name. When Dunmorrow had appeared at Ardley, Dee might have taken the opportunity of getting Anthony under his roof, whilst he sought help in dealing with the miscreant. That would explain Sir Christmas's extraordinary suggestion that the earl should come and stay, with Lady Imelda. Others had been invited to make it appear no more than a pleasant house-party, creating no suspicions in the earl's mind. Whether Dunmorrow had really wanted Ardley, or had already discovered that Dee knew of his crime, was another thing.

She clenched her hands in her lap, trying to be rational

and not letting her awful thoughts run away with her. The fact that Dunmorrow had been across the Irish Sea at the end of last year did not mean he had done away with the unfortunate family man. Yet he was the Marquis of Ashbourne's son: Rosamond had told Davina that, and now Dee was nowhere to be found.

She had never felt so low in all her life as at that moment, and the fear she was harbouring forced her to be brutally honest with herself.

She hated the earl; who wouldn't? But she found him the most attractive man she had ever met, and worse. She had fallen in love with him. It was totally ridiculous, of course, but Davina couldn't deny it any longer. In the present circumstances she had no choice but to face facts.

There was nothing to be done about it, for even if her unspoken accusations were false he was to marry Imelda. She spared a moment of sympathy for Lord Russell's daughter. She and Peter were in love too, but whilst Davina would release Guildford she doubted very much if the earl would be so accommodating as far as Imelda was concerned.

There was no question of marriage now for Davina, either to Guildford or any other man. If she couldn't have Anthony, and it was plain that this was so, she would remain a spinster like Rosamond.

It was a bleak prospect and, since everyone was entitled to cry now and then, Davina buried her face in her hands and wept as if her heart would break.

* * *

An hour later, no one would have known that Lady Davina had had a moment's sorrow to contend with. She joined the others in the drawing-room, nodding to the earl and talking very knowledgeably about horses to Sir Elliot.

Her self-control lasted until a footman came to announce

that the Regent's Secretary had arrived, in company with Dr Erasmus Brown.

The Secretary, Sir Christopher Blackstone, was a nicely-rounded man with an exotic taste in waistcoats and a very soothing air. Upon being told by everyone at once of Dee's disappearance and the death of Gunn, he had hushed their questions and worries and had withdrawn with Brown to examine the body.

Davina felt cold again. It was quite remarkable that, on this particular morning, the Regent's emissary should elect to call at Ardley, bringing with him, of all things, a physician. She told herself she was beginning to manufacture situations which didn't exist, and forced herself to listen as Sir Christopher returned.

"A very sad accident," he said in his slow, calm voice. "Poor fellow; not much more than a boy. However, Dr Brown is satisfied, and I shall return later and see to things. No need for any fears, for it wasn't foul play. Just a mishap; nothing more."

Immediately he had finished speaking, Lord Stuart said loudly:

"I'm leaving this very minute. Had enough of this place."

His anger was echoed by Lady Jessica, who had several acid comments to make about people who invited others to stay with them and then left their guests to their own devices.

"We shall go too," said Lady Rosamond with some thankfulness, for she too had had enough of Ardley, what with one thing and another. "There's nothing to keep us here now, and such an atmosphere is most unsuitable for a young girl. I am going to take my niece home."

Davina didn't raise her head. Once they left Ardley, she wouldn't see the earl again. He had made it quite plain that he didn't like her, and in any event she was by no means certain what kind of man he really was.

But Sir Christopher hadn't finished with them.

"Now, my dear Lord Stuart; Lady Jessica ... all of you. I

beg you not to be so precipitate. There is no call to rush off
this very moment."

"There's no call to stay here either." Barminster wasn't
going to be talked out of his plan. "Why shouldn't we go?
Said the feller broke his own neck, didn't you?"

Blackstone nodded.

"Quite so, but there is a very good reason why you
should all stay."

He seemed almost amused as every head turned to him,
placidly helping himself to snuff from a well-worn silver
box.

"Yes, you see the Prince Regent has expressed a wish to
see Ardley, and has said that he will visit it within the next
day or two. This being so, if you were all to leave, his
highness could not but think such action a slight upon him.
I am sure you would not wish to cause offence; any of you."

The heavy-lidded eyes moved over the amazed faces, the
corners of Sir Christopher's mouth curling upwards.

"Yes, I thought so. His highness will be gratified that you
will be here to receive him, and as for Sir Christmas." He
was comforting, full of solace. "I have questioned the
servants carefully, and understand that their master, who is
growing old and absent-minded, often goes away for a day
or two without warning. He will soon be back; you will see.
There is nothing for any of you to worry about."

He bowed, and turned to the earl.

"My lord, a word in private, if you will. The gardens, I
think."

Davina watched them go, oblivious to the excitement
which was raging round her. Dee's absence, and a dead
footman, had been dismissed from everyone's mind at the
thought of a visit from Prinny, Lady Jessica and Rosamond
unbending towards one another sufficiently to discuss what
they would wear on such an auspicious occasion.

Davina knew that she should have been relieved. If one of
the Regent's own physicians had pronounced Gunn's death
an accident, there was no need to fret on that score any

longer. Sir Christopher's conviction that Dee would soon be back was based on sound fact: the old man did tend to wander off.

Yet the worries wouldn't go. The earl was a man of considerable influence; his father, the marquis, a great friend of the Regent's, so Rosamond had said. Why should Sir Christopher and Dr Brown appear at that precise moment, unless they knew something was wrong? Had they been sent by the Regent himself to help the Earl of Dunmorrow? Certainly St. Romer was the only one whom Blackstone wished to speak to in private.

But until she was sure, she would give the earl the benefit of the doubt, taking care to deal with him cautiously. It would be fatal if he saw her suspicions; even worse if he detected the other emotion in her.

It wouldn't be easy, and it was with a heavy heart that she rose at Rosamond's call and went over to discuss the wholly unimportant subject of ball-gowns.

* * *

"My lord," said Sir Christopher as he and the earl crossed the lawn, "it is imperative that Dee is found."

"Found? I thought you expected him to return at any moment."

"Yes, he may do. It's quite true that this is no new turn of events, but you see, the Regent had asked him to attend upon him at the Pavilion. Sir Christmas didn't arrive."

"When was this? I mean, when should he have been in Brighton?"

"This morning."

The earl's frown deepened.

"Well, it's not very late in the day now, is it? Perhaps he is on his way."

"No, the appointment was for nine o'clock, and Sir Christmas is punctilious in his dealings with the prince. No, he's not on his way to the Pavilion. I thought at first it might be a case of illness; that's why I brought Brown with me. I want you to make enquiries, discreetly, of course. Get Dalzell to help you. There may be nothing to it. There has to be a first time for everything, and perhaps Dee simply did forget.

"What else is likely to have happened to him?" asked the earl when Blackstone appeared to have dismissed the subject completely. "What is it that you are not telling me, sir?"

"Nothing that I can put into words."

"You mean Dee may be dead?"

Blackstone was cryptic.

"It is possible, but better dead in England than alive in another place."

"I don't understand you."

Blackstone cleared his throat.

"No, my dear Dunmorrow, I don't suppose you do. Search the house and grounds well, but don't let anyone except Sir Elliot know that you're doing so. We think he may still be alive."

"We?"

"What exceptionally good weather we're having, aren't we? It is a pleasure to be in such a delightful spot. Yes, we, my lord. Find him; there may not be much time."

It was obvious that the earl was not going to learn any more from the close-mouthed Secretary, but there was one question Anthony had to ask.

"Concerning Robert Gunn. Is what Dr Brown said true? Was it an accident?"

"I'm not a medical man." Sir Christopher stopped to smell a deep-red rose. "We shall have to accept his word, shan't we? And now let's go inside again. It's been a very interesting morning; yes, very interesting indeed."

Four

Elliot listened to Anthony's account of his talk with Blackstone, willing enough to help, but expressing doubts as to their likely success.

"To-night, I shall begin to search the house," said the earl. "There are numerous places where he could be hidden. I'll leave you to look in the outhouses, barns and the like, but don't let anyone see you."

"I shan't." Elliot was brief. "Don't worry about that, but don't expect to find Dee either. Why on earth should he hide in his own house? Are you sure this man Blackstone is not as crazy as Dee himself?"

By then they had joined the others. Lady Rosamond and Jessica were still in a euphoric state at the prospect of the Regent's visit, and had quite buried any previous animosity between them, as they discussed the merits of blue ribbon against jade, and which fan would be most suitable with cream gauze.

Lord Stuart, on the other hand, had no time for the Regent, holding his highness personally responsible for the money he had lost. However, he wasn't such a fool as to leave Ardley and incur royal displeasure: he merely sat by himself and rumbled of his discontent.

Peter and Imelda were by the doors leading to the terrace. The confusion going on around them hardly seemed to impinge on the consciousness, for all they could see was each other.

"What are we going to do?" asked Imelda, her worried

eyes on Peter's face, which she had come to love so much in
such a short space of time. "What will Lady Davina say,
and the earl?"

"I don't know." Peter had lain awake the previous night,
turning the matter over in his mind. "It will be difficult, I
know, but they must be told. It's unthinkable that you
should marry Dunmorrow."

"Or you, Lady Davina. Did you love her once?"

He smiled and took her hand.

"Dearest, no. I thought I did, but it was mere fondness. I
didn't know what love was really like until I saw you alight
from your carriage. Sweetest, you will have to be brave, you
know that?"

"I promise I will be." She managed a vestige of a smile
for him. "If you stay close to me, I shall be courageous."

After a second or two they glanced over their shoulders
and then slipped into the garden. Davina watched them go
without emotion. Until she met Anthony, she had thought
that love at first sight was only to be found in the pages of a
romantic book, but now she knew differently. Poor Peter,
and poor Imelda. She also felt extremely sorry for herself.

"It appears that you have been deserted."

She jumped, for Dunmorrow had come up upon her so
silently that she hadn't been aware of his presence until he
spoke. She was flustered, afraid that he might have been
able to read her thoughts, which was, of course, quite
nonsensical. She noted the ironic glint in his eye and
composed herself.

"You too, my lord."

"Yes, but I shan't lose any sleep over it."

Davina felt sorrier still for Imelda. Even though the girl
was now in love with Peter, the earl's indifference was
scarcely flattering.

"No, I don't suppose you will."

"We must comfort each other, at least, on those
occasions when we are on speaking terms."

"Thank you." She was quite herself again, putting aside

her darker fears about him. "However, I don't need comfort. And I don't keep Peter on a lead."

"Very broadminded of you, but if you were betrothed to me I should keep a very tight rein on you, and you certainly wouldn't be permitted to wander in the gardens with a strange man."

"Permitted?" Wrath made her eyes as bright as diamonds. "I do as I please, and I'm not betrothed to you."

"No, but thank you for saying it as if you wished you were."

She rose, trying to stop the ache inside herself.

"It seems to me," she managed finally, "that you can never resist the opportunity of making me uncomfortable. Why you should wish to make a butt of me, I cannot think. As to your last remark, I shall not comment on that, for it doesn't deserve a second's attention. Now, will you please go away? I find your presence offensive."

"You have foresworn the truth again," he said. "I told you before ... oh my God!"

She turned to stare at him, wondering at the abrupt change in his tone and the stricken expression on his face. Then she became aware that a man was being ushered into the room, the flunkey's bow low and obsequious. The earl appeared to be praying for a miracle, the kind in which the earth would open and swallow him up, as the newcomer spoke.

"... and, as I said, I felt weary, saw this house and decided to seek rest for a while. Thank you; here, take this for your trouble."

Francis St. Romer, Marquis of Ashbourne, nodded to the footman, who bent almost double as he backed out of the room, gleefully clutching a golden guinea.

Anthony watched his father approach with a feeling of apprehension mingled with genuine dread. The marquis looked severe in the extreme. Very tall and lean, with grey hair curled negligently about a well-shaped head, he had light blue eyes, gaunt cheeks and a thin, high-bridged nose.

The mouth, in repose, gave no warning of the quality of his smile, which was gentle, kind and unexpectedly heart-warming to those upon whom he bestowed it. Indeed, his general appearance was wholly and bewilderingly misleading, as the assembled company was soon to discover.

He claimed to have no idea how old he was, but his valet, Gilmer, if pressed, would venture the opinion that his master was no more than in his early fifties. The clothes the marquis wore were vastly expensive, fashioned by the finest tailors in London, yet, despite Gilmer's efforts, it was as if he had donned them for decency's sake only, and had then forgotten all about them.

Whilst cherishing a sincere love for him, the earl had no doubt at all that his father was exceedingly peculiar, if not positively mad. The latter's escapades kept Dunmorrow in a state of spasmodic tension, whenever he was unwise enough to think about his sire, and every day he expected to hear he had lost his revered parent in the latest of his lunatic pursuits.

He gritted his teeth, remembering the wager his father had accepted not ten days before. A race from London to York, against six men half his age, with twice as much ambition to make a name for themselves, and a burning desire to claim the rich prize. The earl had rushed to the capital to put an end to the folly, only to find that the contestants had already gone. Cursing, he had made for the North, delayed by a lame horse, arriving in the fair city of York to discover that the race was long since over, that his father had won with unruffled ease and was challenging his companions to a gallop back to town.

For a long time it had been a mystery to Dunmorrow that his father retained the friendship and deep affection of the Regent, to say nothing of many other influential men and women into the bargain. In the end, he had come to the conclusion that close association with Ashbourne gave them all a smug and satisfying reassurance of their own sanity.

His lordship paused, raising his quizzing-glass. The earl had an awful premonition that the marquis was about to ask who he was and whether they had met before. It would be extremely awkward to explain to one's father in public the exact nature of their relationship, but he braced himself for the task with as much aplomb as he could muster.

Then Ashbourne smiled and, as always, Anthony felt his taut nerve-ends relax. It was the strangest sensation, as if one were being caressed and comforted; even blessed. He bowed formally and the marquis said lightly:

"My dear boy, how splendid! But it is amazing to find you here, since it is only two days ago that I saw you off on your journey to Lisbon."

Anthony sighed. Things hadn't improved.

"That was your brother, sir, although I'm beginning to wish it had been me."

"Really?" The pencilled brows rose a fraction, his lordship's expression unreadable. "Well, yes; can't say I blame you. Pleasant sort of city, Lisbon. As I told that flunkey out there, I'm just on my way to the West Country, but thought I'd rest here for a while, if whoever owns the place doesn't object."

"Break your journey from Bath to the West Country, here, in Sussex?"

The marquis looked lovingly at his son.

"Did I say Bath? Well, no matter. Now, tell me, who are all these delightful people?" The eye-glass moved speculatively over Davina, lips curving appreciatively. "Yes, indeed! Who is this divine goddess?"

Temporarily defeated, the earl performed the introductions, marvelling, as he usually did on such occasions, that the small group was glowing with pleasure, instead of fleeing to their respective rooms, where they would be safe for an hour or two. It was really quite extraordinary the effect his father had on even the most sensible of people.

"And dear Louisa." Ashbourne made an elegant leg,

kissing Rosamond Temple's hand with a flourish. "You are as lovely as ever."

"Don't be absurd, Francis," said Davina's aunt crossly. "You know perfectly well that my name is Rosamond, not Louisa. You've known it for thirty years or more. Really! Your memory gets worse every time I see you."

Her hand was still imprisoned in the marquis's, and Davina watched in fascination as Rosamond's annoyance turned to something very like a simper.

"It's all this detail, you know. Can't remember names too well, but I always recognise beauty. We must talk later. Louisa; I shall look forward to it."

The earl steered his father away, trying to explain the absence of Christmas Dee and the proposed visit of the Regent. He was in the middle of begging his father to understand that it wasn't his royal highness who had fallen down the cellar stairs, when Peter and Imelda returned.

They looked like a pair of rosy school-children, caught in the act of a piece of mischief for which they knew they would get a scolding, but Davina could see more in them than that, and it was as if a hand had squeezed her heart.

She would release Peter, of course, but would the earl be so obliging? He seemed a good deal more human and less patronizing now that his father had arrived, but he could still be responsible for terrible deeds which she didn't wish to think about.

"Well," said the marquis, "perhaps Sir Christmas needed a change of air. Can't always stay in one spot, can one? Don't understand what George was doing in the basement, but I hope his fall wasn't a bad one. Not the age or shape to go tumbling about like that. Ah, and who is this?"

The earl raised his eyes to heaven and, in spite of everything, Davina began to enjoy herself. She had taken an instant liking to the marquis and the effect of his presence on his wretched offspring was remarkable. If she, Davina, couldn't squash the earl, his father was more than capable of doing so, and in the most disarming of ways.

"My betrothed, sir; Lady Imelda Russel. And this is Sir Peter Guildford, who is to marry Lady Davina."

It was useless to remind his father that he knew Imelda quite well, and the fact that he had to announce that the foppish Guildford was going to wed Davina Temple left a sour taste in his mouth. Then he became aware of the looks the two of them were exchanging and, despite his preoccupation with keeping his own wits on an even keel, a ray of hope shone through his black thoughts.

Yet was it really possible that the two of them, as coy as a pair of turtle-doves, could have fallen in love so rapidly? He almost laughed aloud, but he wasn't amused. It was wholly possible; he had known he was in love with the shrewish but quite bewitching Davina from the moment he had met her.

"So, you two are to marry, are you?" The marquis had taken one of Peter's hands in his, the other holding Imelda's, as if about to join them in matrimony there and then. "Yes, a very nice young beau, m'dear. You should be well-suited, and it's clear enough what you feel for each other."

There was silence in the room, the company digesting a fact which it hadn't noticed before, Rosamond mumbling a few words to the marquis's discredit. Really, Francis was quite impossible, and now he was causing fresh difficulties by imagining Imelda Russell was in love with Guildford. She took another look at the two of them and then heaved a sigh.

Of course, Francis was right as usual, but what confusion it was going to cause! She glanced at her niece, but Davina wasn't giving anything away.

"Dear God," said the earl under his breath. "Is it worth trying again?"

Davina had moved to his side and now she gave a quiet laugh.

"I don't think it is."

"Neither do I."

He took her arm, as the conversation became general again, leading her into a corner away from the others.

"I'm sorry if this has caused you embarrassment. I think I should tell you about my father."

"Yes?"

She was still amused, conscious that her previous anger and unhappiness had lifted. There was something about the marquis's presence which made the world seem safe, and on its right course again. She couldn't put the reasons for this feeling into words: it was simply a fact, and she accepted it gratefully.

"Well, he is rather eccentric. In fact, one might be forgiven for thinking him demented."

"I don't find him so." She was artless. "And his manners are beyond reproach."

"Unlike mine, as no doubt you were about to add."

"Not at all," she returned blithely. Whether he was innocent or guilty, the earl was very close to her, and it was a precious moment. "There is no point in stating the obvious. Tell me, does your father really think that Lady Imelda is going to marry Peter?"

"Probably." He couldn't imagine why he'd ever asked for Imelda's hand, but he hadn't known then of the existence of the girl whose wide hazel eyes were on his, and whose proximity was making his pulse race again. "Before we know it, he'll have the pair of them at the altar."

"I do hope not." She assumed a serious and wholly false expression. "I really do hope it doesn't come to that. I shouldn't like you to die of a broken heart."

His lips twitched.

"My patience has been tried sufficiently for one afternoon; be careful."

"Will you mind very much? I'm not teasing you now."

Their eyes met again and Davina felt quite light-headed.

"No, I shan't mind at all. Will you?"

She wanted to say no, very loudly, and put her arms round him, but the risk was too great. She wasn't sure what he had done, but she was well aware that if she behaved in such an unfashionable manner he would put her down with a cutting remark which would make her want to weep again.

"No, I had already come to the conclusion that Peter and I were unsuited."

"Poor Davina." He wasn't prepared to be the first to move either, and his voice was mocking. "I was right; we shall have to console each other, you know."

"I doubt if I shall have time." She was relieved to find her equilibrium had returned, the danger of making a fool of herself having passed. "But I'm sure that Lady Jessica would be glad to offer you solace in your loss."

The earl raised her hand to his lips and suddenly she found the battle of words palled terribly. His kiss was more than perfunctory, and it made her whole body tingle, as if she had only just come alive. She wanted to draw her fingers away, but he was holding her spellbound.

Then he released her, watching her from under half-closed lids.

"Don't play games with me, madam, unless you want to get burnt. Worse, you might find that my father has arranged a double wedding, and you'd end up in my bed, and you wouldn't like that, would you? Tied for life to a man you hate."

"I don't hate you."

She had blurted the words out before she could stop herself, overcome with confusion. She wished that she were a hundred miles away, and had never met this unfeeling brute who knew so well how to inflict hurt.

She waited for the next lash of his tongue, but nothing happened. When she finally managed to raise her head, he flicked her cheek gently with one forefinger.

"I know you don't; I've always known that. Perhaps a

double wedding wouldn't be such a bad thing after all. It would be an excellent solution to our dilemma, don't you agree?''

"Dilemma?" Her face felt scorched where he had touched it, the softness of his tone like music in her ears. "What dilemma?"

"Why," he returned in some surprise. "We would both have Ardley then, wouldn't we?"

"Oh! You ... you ... are quite insufferable! And I've changed my mind; I do hate you after all. Indeed, I absolutely abominate you!"

He left her, humming to himself, feeling a sense of marvellous well-being, despite what was going on about him. When this muddle had been cleared up, the taming of Lady Davina Temple would be a lot of fun – for both of them.

*   *   *

Below stairs, the servants were having their own problems. The marked change in the demeanour, noticed by several of the guests, had not been due to a fear of a ghost, but by the formidable presence of Horace Codder.

A boot-boy, searching for a lost brush, had been foolhardy enough to enter upon Codder's refuge and had nearly died of fright when a bony hand clutched at his throat.

In no time at all, Codder had summoned the whole boiling of them to his hidy-hole, as if he were master of Ardley, and they his slaves. Indeed, the servants soon discovered that that was precisely what they were: Codder's slaves.

"Now understand this," – Horace had been menacing – "the lot o' yer. One word to them upstairs, and yer own mothers wouldn't knows yer as they wrapped yer in yer winding-sheets."

"But ... who ... who are you, and what are you doing

here?'' Rourke had felt it was incumbent upon him to make some sort of stand, but had found himself on the floor, nursing a bruised jaw for his pains. ''Ah! I only meant ...''

''Shut yer potato-trap unless yer wants yer teeth knocked down yer wind-pipe. Now, listen. Me and me friend 'ere wants food, regular like. Wine and beer too. Any funny business, and I'll 'ave yer insides out with me knife.''

Looking at the wicked blade, there hadn't been one of the trembling minions who had disbelieved Horace, their quivering fear turning to panic later, when Robert Gunn had been found dead near to where Smythe and Codder were hiding. None of them had thought Robert had met with an accident, despite what that pompous doctor had said. They dared not ask Codder if he had been responsible, but such a question was superfluous. Who else would have done it?

None of the staff had mentioned to Codder that Sir Christmas had gone. Whispering timidly amongst themselves, glancing over their shoulders every now and then to see if the dreadful man who looked like a living skeleton had crept along the passage, they had agreed it was best to say nothing. If the two monsters thought there was no master in the establishment, their demands might grow worse.

The commotion caused by Robert's death hadn't gone unnoticed by Horace. He had seen a new paralysed glaze in the servants' eyes; heard unusual comings and goings when he had opened his door a crack. Having extracted every last ounce of information from Rourke, he had turned to Smythe in some perplexity.

''Funny. Didn't lay a finger on 'im, so I wonders 'oo did 'im in. Best let that lot along there think it were me. Keep 'em in order, like.''

Later, Rourke had told Codder of the visit of the two important men, one a physician, who had pronounced Gunn's death an accident.

Codder had given the butler a significant look.

"Very nice and neat, but you and me know different, don't we? Didn't tell 'em about us, did yer?"

"No, no, I swear we didn't!"

"No, don't suppose yer did, or they'd 'ave come fer us before now. Well, just remember what I've said. There could be other accidents, yer know. Now 'op it. Git me some wine and a bit o' that fruit pie. I likes that."

Once again, the servants had crowded round the large kitchen table, but their collective nerve was broken. It was evident that the awesome being along in the storeroom had been responsible for Gunn's end, and not one of them doubted that he'd killed Sir Christmas too, without realising that he had been the owner of Ardley.

Briefly, they had considered approaching the earl, but had soon dismissed the idea. Codder would find out somehow. To them, he was omniscient and, although Dunmorrow was a fine, brave buck, Horace was more to be feared, and they had obeyed his demand for silence.

"Told yer, didn't I?" Horace had been complacent. "Blasted fools upstairs thought it were a mishap, but them lot down 'ere knows it weren't. They think it were me. That'll keep 'em quiet. You listenin', Mortimer?"

Smythe, pleasantly bleary with too much claret and game pie, had made appropriate noises.

"That's right, me lad." Horace had been tucking himself in the new blanket which Biddy had been forced to find for him. "Just you stay with me, and you'll be as safe as 'ouses."

"Wass the time?" Smythe had opened one eye, too drunk to continue praising his companion. "Can't tell if it's day or night down 'ere in this 'ole."

"What yer want to know the time fer?" Horace had spat on the floor. "It's late, that's all yer need ter know. Now keep quiet and go to sleep."

"Yes, Horace."

Smythe had slid down the wall until he was flat on the floor. His stomach was full, his mind befuddled. Horace was right. It didn't matter what the time was, and their situation was much better than he had dared hope it would be.

A minute or two later he had been snoring, and Codder had composed himself for sleep, well-pleased with the turn of events. A cosy and safe place, so no reason to go on the run for a while. As he drifted off, he had planned what he would have for breakfast, and how to entice Esther Thrussel, one of the chambermaids, into revealing more of her ample charms. Yes, all said and done, it had been a good move, and Horace had turned on his side and fallen sound asleep.

* * *

Just after one o'clock, the earl took a candle and went to look in Dee's bedroom. He had intended to go straight to the basement, but it occurred to him that the servants might have missed something in their master's chamber which would give a clue to his whereabouts.

The room was very dark, one flickering light not much use in the stygian gloom. Anthony moved very quietly, opening a large chest and feeling the contents with one hand. There was a cupboard in one corner, but Dee wasn't in it, nor was he lurking behind the heavy drapes at the windows. Of course, Elliot had been quite right: why on earth should Dee hide in his own house?

Dunmorrow moved to the bed, unslept in, as the servants had said. He was about to turn away when he caught a glimpse of something white. He knelt for a minute, just staring at the handkerchief, which had been almost concealed by the bed-frill. The blood on the kerchief was not in small spots, but in large, ugly stains. Then he rose. It was no good staying there and it was time he got downstairs.

As he went out into the corridor, his discovery still in his hand, he found himself face to face with the marquis, armed with a five-branch candle-stick. He knew it was useless to ask his father what he was doing there, and he didn't particularly want to raise the subject, in case the marquis posed a similar question as to his son's activities.

But Ashbourne seemed to find nothing unusual about meeting Anthony in the dead of night, coming out of the room of a man who had vanished into thin air.

"Cut yourself, Dunmorrow?" The lazy eyes hadn't missed the stains. "Should be more careful. Heard this house is to be sold. Thinking of buying it for your bride, that charmer, Davina Temple? Splendid idea."

"Not Lady Davina." Rapidly the early stuffed the white linen square into his pocket, hoping his father would forget about it. "I'm to marry Imelda Russell."

His voice was uncertain. He knew that he would never love anyone but Davina, and not so many hours before he had had comforting reassurance that her feelings towards him were far from what she claimed them to be. Since then, however, he had had time to think, and it was going to be the very devil of a task to get matters sorted out. His earlier pleasure at the idea of bringing Davina to heel had since been tempered by the strong possibility that Lord Russell might not care for Sir Peter as a son-in-law.

Guildford was well-bred enough, but he wasn't a rich man, and Russell, a very eminent personage, had a high opinion of himself and his family. Then there was the Earl of Hillborough to consider. He too might raise objections about his child's wedding a notorious rake, instead of the compliant, inoffensive boy to whom he had agreed to entrust his daughter's future.

"Never heard of her."

"What?"

Anthony's attention had been wandering along unhappy paths, but his father's words jerked him back to the present.

"This Imelda girl you spoke of a minute ago. Don't know her."

The earl steeled himself to be patient.

"You have only just renewed your acquaintance with her, don't you remember? She came in from the garden with Peter Guildford. Also, you approved my marriage to her. You even discussed the matter with her father."

"Did I? Can't say I recall it. So, that was Imelda Russell, was it? Pretty child, but too clinging."

Anthony could feel his choler raising. He wished to God his father would go to bed, so that he himself could then get down to the basement to continue his search.

"Clinging?"

"Yes, nothin more infuriatin' than a gel who's forever holding on to one's arm like she was doing to what's-his-name."

"Guildford."

"Yes, if you say so. Very irritating: quite ruins a man's aim when he's about to take a shot at someone."

"That is probably a good thing." The earl was short. "And now if you will excuse me ..."

"They'll make a good match though." The marquis nodded sagely. "Boy's uncertain of himself, and she'll help him to feel important, don't you see? Some men like that sort of thing. Anyway, I hope you and Davina will be happy."

"Good-night, sir," said the earl with quiet violence, and made for his own room. "I trust that you will sleep well."

The marquis watched him go, the glow from the candles shewing a faint smile on his lips as his son melted into the darkness.

"Well, well," he said to himself as he heard the earl's door close none too quietly. "Anthony in love. Whoever would have thought that of him? Damned boy makes me feel quite old. I'll be a grandfather before I know it."

Five

Codder was dreaming of the luscious Esther. She was warm and unresisting in his arms, and he was about to demand the ultimate of her, when something with a kick like a mule shattered his happy slumber.

He shot up with a ripe oath, knocking his head on the wall.

"What's the matter with yer, yer bloody fool?" he demanded. "Smythe, I'll 'ave yer ..."

He broke off, sinking back as the last strands of sleep left him, along with the shade of Esther. Mortimer was gibbering in his own corner and there was a light in the room: a lantern perched on the table which the servants had brought along for the use of their unwanted guests.

Then Horace's gaze took in the man standing over them. The cut of his coat, and perfection of his smallclothes, proclaimed him a dandy, but it wasn't those, or the shining Hessians, with which Codder was concerned.

It was the steady hand, holding a pistol, aimed at his head, and the expression in the green eyes which Horace was worried about. He'd known a lot of men in his time and was quick to sum up his fellow-beings. This one was dangerous and not to be trifled with.

"Stay where you are." The earl's voice was soft, but Horace didn't misread that either. "If you move a finger, I'll shoot it off."

Codder ignored Mortimer's frenzied twittering. He needed to concentrate on the newcomer, if he were to stay alive.

"''Oo are you?" he managed finally. "What yer doin' down 'ere?"

"I was going to ask you the self-same thing." Anthony was considering the long, emaciated body. It wasn't hard now to see why the servants had at first thought they'd seen a ghost, nor was it likely that they hadn't found the two men by this time. No wonder they were frightened out of their wits. "Who are you, and what have you done with Sir Christmas Dee? I'd also like to know why you killed Robert Gunn. Did he see you make away with Dee?"

Codder stopped gawping. There were some very funny things going on, but he wasn't going to be blamed for what he hadn't done, nor accused of killing someone he didn't know.

"'Ere, wait a minute." He half-rose, stopping as the gun moved a fraction closer. "'Orl right, 'orl right; I ain't goin' ter git up. I'll give yer no trouble, but I've never 'eard of Dee, or whatever yer called 'im, and I swears on me mother's grave I didn't touch Gunn."

"Liar!" The earl moved so swiftly that Codder was taken completely by surprise. "Tell me the truth, or you'll get more of that."

Horace's head was jangling like a peal of cracked bells. He'd been right in his judgment about this man, whose fist had struck with the force of a cannon-ball.

"Mother of God!" He shook himself out of his dizziness. "'Ere, no need fer that. I ain't done a thing, at least, not what yer says I've done. Me and Mortimer 'ere are as innocent as new-born babes."

He let out a loud cry as the earl's foot caught him in a particularly painful spot.

"Christ! Stop it, stop it! I tells yer we've done nothin'. Never 'eard of this man what yer talkin' about. 'Oo is 'e?"

"You're in his house, you numskull." Dunmorrow's voice was like vitriol. "He is missing, and one of his footmen is dead. Do you seriously expect me to believe that you're not responsible?"

"I tells yer we're not!" Codder was still doubled up in agony. "We got in 'ere, 'cos we're on the run. Mortimer and me got out of Stockland Gaol a day or so back. Gawd, I feels bad."

"You'll feel a good deal worse if you don't tell me the truth."

"I'm tellin' yer the truth, I swears I am. Yes, we're convicts, Smythe and me. We was ter be transported, see, and we didn't fancy that, so we ran orf. First, we 'id in one of them buildings outside. When we realised it were part of an 'ouse, we thought we was done fer, but then we found a trap-door and came down 'ere, but we've 'armed no one."

"You've terrorized the servants."

Dunmorrow didn't take his eyes off Codder, but he was beginning to believe him. A desperate felon, but there was a certain ring of truth about his words.

"You admit that?"

Codder shrugged, unrepentent.

"Well, we was 'ungry, and them's a feeble lot."

"Feeble enough for you to kill one of them?"

"No! I tells yer ..."

"Don't bother." The earl gestured Codder to be quiet. "I'm tired of your protestations."

"Me what?"

"Never mind. I'll accept for the moment that you didn't kill the footman, and you say you don't know Dee? You've never seen him, since you've been here?"

"Never." Horace was emphatic. "Only ones we've seen 'ave bin that daft lot along there. 'Ere, yer goin' to give us up?"

Dunmorrow was thoughtful. His efforts to find Sir Christmas had so far been wholly unproductive. He couldn't even mention the matter to anyone except Elliot, and Elliot was a stranger to Dee and his household. The servants had sworn they had no idea where their master was, but one of them at least could have been lying. If Dee had been taken by force, then someone in the house must have been in on the conspiracy.

These two might help, and the cold green eyes turned back to Codder.

"No, not yet, provided that you agree to assist me."

"Anythin', sir, anythin'. Horace's relief made him expansive in his offer. "What yer want us ter do? Twist a neck or two? Do it in a trice. No trouble at all."

"Certainly not. Indeed, if you so much as lay a hand on anyone in this house, guest or servant, I shall cut your throat myself."

Mortimer was pasty-white.

"Jesus God! Horace, I said ..."

"Shut up!" Codder turned an ingratiating smile on the earl. "What was it yer wanted then, yer lordship? Bit o' robbery?"

"No. Be quiet and listen to what I'm saying, because if you don't you are likely to find yourselves back at Stockland, buried in the yard."

Mortimer gulped and even Codder felt real alarm. As he'd surmised, this was a tricky customer.

"First," said the earl, "you will not mention to anyone that I've been here. No one at all; is that understood?"

They nodded, still wary of the pistol, and the earl's boot which could half-cripple a man.

"Good. Then I want you to question the servants about Dee. Naturally, we have already made our own enquiries, but they all swear they know nothing. Their master tends to go off now and then without warning, but this time I don't think he did. It is possible that one of his staff helped in the matter of his disappearance, and is now lying. I want to know if that is so."

"Right yer are. I'll screw it out o' 'em."

"You'll do no such thing. You'll frighten them all into deeper silence. That's not the way to do it, you imbecile. Ask them a few things, but casually. An odd question here, another there. Try to gain their confidence, or at least the confidence of one of them."

The earl gave Codder an unpleasant smile.

"Doubtless you've had your way with one of the maids by now."

Horace didn't bother to protest his innocence in that direction, seeing it was pointless.

"Not yet, yer lordship, but there's one I've got me eye on."

"Good, then make a fuss of her. Treat her gently, and get her talking, and if you rape her I'll see you never again have a desire for a woman. Do I make myself clear?"

"Aye." The vision of Esther's white body, soft and yielding against his own, was banished from Codder's reluctant mind. "Whatever yer says."

"By the way, who are you? What are your full names?"

When they told him, the earl nodded.

"Very well, Master Codder and Master Smythe. Help me, and I'll help you. You have my oath that I won't mention to anyone that you are here."

"No one? Yer promises that?"

"I have given my word." Dunmorrow was frosty. "Your word may not mean much to you, but mine is a yardstick of my honour. No one at all will learn of your presence, provided that you do as you're told."

He made for the door.

"I shall be back before long to hear what you've learned. Remember, I haven't been here, and you are not to molest anyone. God help you if you do."

Smythe shuddered as the door closed behind Anthony.

"What we goin' ter do? 'E won't keep 'is promise to the likes of us. 'E'll give us away."

Codder was still rubbing that part of his anatomy where the earl's boot had done its work. A visit from a man like that was the last thing he'd expected, and he had no illusions about the threats made by the intruder. Still, it could have been worse. They could have been discovered by someone who hadn't wanted a job done, and questioning Esther would be pleasant enough, even if he couldn't bring all his dreams to fruition.

"No," he said after a pause. "'e won't do that, not 'im. 'E's given 'is word, and that's good enough fer me. Now git back ter sleep, will yer."

"It's rum, ain't it, Horace? This man goin' off like that. Master of the 'ouse."

"Aye, its a queer turn. Somethin's 'appened to 'im, that's fer sure. Man like the one what was just 'ere don't git agitated fer nothin'. I'll 'ave a word with Esther in the mornin'. Now shut up, will yer? I've 'ad enough gabbin' fer one night."

*   *   *

The following morning, Davina went for a walk in the gardens. She saw Peter and Imelda disappearing amongst the trees and it filled her with gloom. It wasn't that she wanted Guildford at her own side; in fact, that was the very last thing she hankered for. But if there were someone else to walk with ...

"What a thing it is to be young and in love!"

Davina turned, startled by the unexpected voice.

"My lord, I didn't hear you coming."

"Then I crave your forgiveness, my dear." The marquis sketched a bow. "It was not my intention to make you jump, but I was forced to the observation, seeing those two together. I am so old, you see, that I have almost forgotten what passion is like."

Davina gave a rather unhappy smile.

"I don't believe that."

She tried to dispel her misery, but the kindness she saw in the marquis's eyes mader her own fill with tears.

Ashbourne handed her a handkerchief edged with expensive lace, smelling very faintly of a light perfume.

"Don't worry," he advised gently. "They'll marry one another; you'll see."

She sniffed, wholly unconvinced.

"Peter is engaged to me, but I don't love him. Of course, I have a fondness for him, but that isn't love."

"As you have only just discovered." Ashbourne patted her hand. "Never mind, it'll all work out. Things have a way of getting out of perspective at your age. When you are ancient like me, nothing seems worth fretting about."

"Possibly not, but that's such a long time for me to wait to find out ... oh!" She was horrified. "My lord, I intended no insult. I pray you to forgive my thoughtless words."

He laughed, highly amused.

"There's nothing to forgive, and you have no need to be concerned. Your tribulations won't last that long."

"I fear they may do. I shall have to wed Peter. I've told my father and my aunt, and, indeed, everyone, that I insist on having him, and ..."

"... you are too pig-headed to admit you were wrong?"

She hung her head.

"It will be difficult, but it's not only that. Yes, of course I shall have to admit it, for Peter's sake. He and Imelda are made for each other."

"You suffer the pangs of envy watching them?"

"Yes, I have to confess that I do."

"You are refreshingly honest for a woman." The marquis was regarding her with approval. "Most females of my acquaintance would never make such an admission. Yes, it's all very convenient. You are not the only one I know who is pig-headed and bluntly truthful. And, of course, the children will be quite delightful."

Davina watched him walk away. Disjointed though the marquis's comments were, she had known at once what he meant, but the realisation brought more tears.

Setting aside for the moment the problem of Peter, and her own love for Anthony St. Romer, she felt bound to ask herself why Ashbourne had come to Ardley at all, if not to help his son. And, if he had come for that purpose, he would be more concerned with spiriting the earl out of England than in assisting him to discard Imelda Russell.

She tucked the handkerchief away, her sorrow with it. She wasn't such a weakling that she would die if she couldn't have the man she wanted, but life would be so very long and boring without him.

She sighed, and turned back to the house to find Rosamond. The sooner she learned how to act like a spinster the better, for that was what she would be until the day she died.

"Damn you, my lord," she said under her breath, as she reached the terrace. "Why did I ever have to meet you? Damn you a thousand times for what you've done to me."

* * *

"What do you mean, you found it by the front door?"

Dunmorrow's tone was rough and Ben Jenkins, one of the flunkeys, took a step backwards. His nerves were already in shreds because of Codder and Smythe in the basement, and now the earl looked ready to fell him to the ground.

"Just that ... m'lord. At least, it were Mr Rourke who found the note; left on the step."

"And no one was seen?"

"No one."

"It is midnight now." Dunmorrow became aware of the man's pallor and softened his voice. The servants were having a sufficiently bad time dealing with the felons, to say nothing of the demands of the Marquis of Ashbourne, without having to face his ill-humour as well. "Do you know how long ago it was delivered? When was the last time the door was opened?"

Jenkins breathed again. The young lord was flicking a gold coin between his fingers and it looked extremely promising.

"Not more than fifteen minutes before. Staple, he's another footman, thought he heard a noise outside, and went to look."

"What was it?"

"There wasn't anything there."

"No note?"

"No, sir, I'm sure of that, because when Mr Rourke found that one of the dogs had got into the house he chased it through the front door and then he noticed the letter. Asked us all if we'd heard anyone about, and that's when Staple told him about the sounds."

The coin changed hands and the earl read the note again, whilst Jenkins pocketed his unexpected windfall and returned to the kitchen. There was a perfectly good servants' hall, but since the discovery of Codder the staff had tended to huddle together in the kitchen where they felt tolerably safe, comforted by the smell of cooking, warmed by the stove.

The instructions in the letter were brief. Dunmorrow was to be at Cheshire House by two o'clock, bringing with him a thousand guineas, if he wanted to see Sir Christmas alive again. He was also to go alone.

The earl cursed softly, but at least it was confirmation that Dee hadn't left Ardley willingly, a fact which had become ominously apparent to Anthony by then.

He went along to Elliot's room, the latter immediately proclaiming his intention of accompanying the earl.

"You can't. Look at the letter again. I'm to go alone. To ignore that might mean Dee's death. Now where in heaven's name is Cheshire House?"

"You can't go alone; it would be foolhardy. I'll keep out of sight."

"No." Dunmorrow waved Dalzell's offer aside. "I'm grateful, but no. However, I'll borrow a thousand guineas from you, if you've got it, for I've nothing like the sum with me."

"Neither have I." Dalzell looked worried. "If you don't take the money, there's a real chance that whoever's holding Dee will kill him."

"I shall take the money; I know where to get it, don't

concern yourself about that. Now, I must find Rourke, or someone, and discover where this place is."

"Be careful." Elliot caught the earl's arm. "I wish you'd change your mind, Anthony. I swear they wouldn't see so much as my shadow."

"I can't take the chance, but thank you."

"Let me know when you get back."

"Yes of course."

The earl found a weary Rourke on the stairs, who told him that Cheshire House was a derelict mansion some five miles away.

"South, m'lord, and then down by Cotswood. Take the Rachet Road, and you can't miss it, for it stands by itself. But you won't find anyone there."

The earl considered the drawn features of the butler, wondering it it were fatigue, fear or guilt which made the man's eyes so shifty.

"I'll find it, and rather think you may be wrong."

Rourke was too tired to unravel what the earl was talking about, for he had had his seventh summons in the last hour to attend upon the Marquis of Ashbourne.

During the day, Anthony had had a look in the barn where the convicts said that they had found the trap-door, and now he used it to descend to the store where Codder and Smythe were hiding. It was safer than going through the house, for some of the servants were still at work.

Codder roused himself, ready to spit his anger at whoever had disturbed him, servile at once when he saw the earl.

"Well, have you asked the questions I told you to ask?"

"Yes, m'lord, and I'd swear that this lot don't know nothin'. I've asked 'em all, and they're like a bunch of babes-in-arms, and that's a fact. Don't reckon they had aught to do with their master's goin'."

"Mm. Well, keep trying." The earl sat on the corner of the table, the letter in his hand. "I've received a demand to go to Cheshire House at two o'clock. I'm to take a thousand guineas, and I'm to go unaccompanied, if I want to see Sir

Christmas alive again. What do you know about that, you unspeakable blackguard?"

Codder's jaw dropped, Smythe struck dumb as usual in the face of trouble.

"It was found on the doorstep, and you have access from the house, haven't you? You could have used the trap-door."

"But I don't know where the place is; may the good Lord strike me down if I lie."

"He probably will," said the earl coldly. "Do you know the Rachet Road, past Cotswood?"

"I've bin there, yes, but ..."

"Then you know the house, you infernal ..."

"No!"

Mortimer was gaping at Codder, who had shrunk back against the wall. Smythe had known Codder for some time, but he'd never seen him afraid of anyone before. Still, the man did have a pistol, and the line of his mouth turned Mortimer's stomach over.

"If I find that you have lied to me, I'll cut your ears off and feed them to the pigs."

"Gawd no!" Codder put dirty hands over the threatened lobes. "Sir, I be tellin' the truth. 'Ow could I 'ave writted ter yer, seein' I don't know 'ow. Never learned; never will now. 'Sides yer 'aven't told us yer name, 'ave yer?"

Dunmorrow considered Codder a moment longer. He was inclined to believe the man. The fear was genuine; the fact that he couldn't form his letters quite believable. He doubted too whether either of them had broken their promise, and tried to find out from the servants who he, Anthony, was.

"Very well." Dunmorrow rose. "For the moment I'll accept what you say, but if you're tricking me, and I find that whoever is at Cheshire House is a friend of yours, you'll not only need a priest; you'll need an undertaker as well."

He went back into the house the way he had come,

entering by a side window. If the felons were telling the truth, whoever had kidnapped Dee had known enough about his household to be aware of his current guests, and address a note to one of them. It wasn't a pleasant thought, but at least whoever it was had shewn his hand at last, and it was a straightforward case of abduction and extortion. With any luck, Sir Christmas would be back in his own bed within an hour or two.

He was just about to go upstairs when he heard a loud noise. A hollow clashing or rattle of some sort; a rumble of wood on wood. It was coming from the direction of the Orangery, and he hurried along the passage leading to that most desirable adjunct to Ardley.

He stopped dead in the doorway, wondering why he had imagined for a second that the disturbance was being created by anyone other than his father. The marquis was playing bowls; thoroughly enjoying himself.

"Hell's teeth, my lord," said Anthony in exasperation, "at this time of night? You'll have the whole house up. The noise is enough to wake the dead."

Ashbourne bent to take aim.

"I'm told the dead are already awake. Shall be damned sorry if I don't see this wraith whilst I'm here. I've nearly finished. After this, I'm going shooting."

"Shooting?" The earl was losing his grip again. "In the dark?"

"Moon's out. Plenty of light."

"Father, I beg you to do no such thing. Think of those who are trying to rest."

"Well, perhaps you're right. Wouldn't want to disturb Louisa. Were you looking for me?"

"I need a thousand guineas," said Anthony, contriving to get between the bowls and his father. "I haven't that much with me, but I thought you might have."

The marquis expressed astonishment that his son should doubt for a moment that he had set out on a journey without proper preparation.

"Never travel with less than ten thousand pounds," he said, straightening up. "What if I should want to buy a string of horses, or see a curricle which takes my eye?"

"Or even come upon a dozen elephants," muttered the earl as he followed his father to the archway leading to the main hall.

As they reached the bottom of the stairs, Anthony swung round quickly. He was quite certain that there had been a sound: he wasn't sure whether it had been a rustle, or a light footstep, but it hadn't been his imagination. There was no sign of movement, and the noise wasn't repeated, but the earl knew that his conversation with his father had been overheard.

The marquis had paused on the first tread, but he didn't turn his head. After a second he continued his ascent, leaving the earl to his worries. It could have been Codder who had come after him, but he doubted it. Perhaps it had been a servant, and no mystery at all.

It was characteristic of the marquis that he had not enquired why his son wanted a large sum of money at that hour of the night, but Anthony felt some explanation was called for.

"I have heard of a place near here, Cheshire House. Rather good as hells go, so they tell me."

The calm blue eyes met his own.

"Really? You must tell me what it's like. May ride over myself another evening. Like a game of chance now and then."

The earl hated deceiving his father. It was true, of course, that he was going to Cheshire House, but it was a ruin, not a gambling-club.

"Yes, I will, sir, and thank you for the loan. I will return it as soon as possible."

He left hastily, making for his room, at the same time as Davina Temple crossed the hall, her face very white.

She hadn't been able to sleep, and when the unearthly noises began she had left her room to see what was going on. At last she had traced the sound to the Orangery, just in time to hear the earl's request to his father, and her heart had taken another knock.

Why should Anthony want such a sum at that hour? There was nothing at Ardley on which he could spend it, unless he was preparing to buy someone's silence.

She hadn't waited to learn more, but had rushed into the library to hide until the coast was clear. Back in her room, she curled up on the window-seat and looked down at the gardens in front of the house. They were bathed in moonlight, but there were also shadows, and she very soon locked her door, to be on the safe side.

She wasn't sure how long she'd been sitting there when she heard the snuffle of a horse and the faint chink of bridle and bit. She leaned cautiously out of the open window, fearful in case the rider should look up and see her.

Then she drew back, full of despair. It had been the earl, she was sure of it. Despite the distance, she had recognised him, as one did when it was the man one loved. It was a sort of sixth sense which she had only recently realised she possessed.

Innocent people slept in their beds at night, but the earl was riding off, hell for leather. It had to be connected with Sir Christmas's disappearance, and Gunn's death. What else would take a man out as late as that?

It was only when she was finally settled in bed that an alternative solution occurred to her, and she sat up abruptly.

"A mistress," she said aloud. "My lord, if that's what it is, I shall never forgive you as long as I live."

Six

Cheshire House was as deserted and desolate as Rourke had warned the earl it would be. It lay well back from the Rachet Road, slumped despondently in its overgrown garden.

The earl tethered his horse away from the gates and began to move towards the house, but there was no light nor sign of life as he got to the front door.

The lantern which he had brought with him illuminated the hall, its floor covered with dust, the walls festooned with cobwebs. He stood there listening, but the place felt empty. He sensed no other human presence, and cursed. A wild goose-chase, or a way of getting him out of Ardley?

When he heard the slight sound outside, he ran down the worn stone steps. It was as if a foot had trodden on a twig and snapped it. The raised lantern revealed nothing, but a second later it fell from his hand as he pitched forward from a blow on the back of his head.

Some ten minutes later consciousness returned, and he half-raised himself, his vision misty. After a moment he became aware of two figures squatting by his side, his hand reaching for his gun.

"No need fer that," Codder whispered. "Weren't us what did this."

Dunmorrow got to his feet, still giddy.

"Then what in the name of Hades are you doing here?"

"I didn't want to come." Smythe was whining. "But Horace said ..."

"I said it were our duty," said Codder unctuously, pushing Mortimer aside. "Since yer lordship didn't give us away, it seemed only right to repay the favour. When yer told us where yer were goin', I thought we ought ter follow yer, just in case, so we borrowed an 'orse."

"The money!"

"Anthony turned baleful eyes on Codder as he found the bag was missing.

"Never worry yerself, sir, 'ere it is, safe and sound."

The earl's head had cleared, and he took the bag, weighing it in his hand.

"It seems that I have misjudged you. My apologies.

"None required. One good turn deserves another, like I said."

"If it wasn't you who hit me, who was it? Did you see anyone?"

"Two of 'em, but not together."

"Two? What do you mean, not together?"

"Well, first there was a man 'oo came out o' them bushes over there. Didn't see 'is face, nor much else of 'im, come ter that. Clouds 'ad covered the moon. 'E were just a shape. Then there were the other."

"You saw him? The second man?"

"Not proper. Wouldn't know 'im again, but just as 'e mounted up clouds passed a bit and we saw the lower part of 'im. Dressed like you, m'lord, very expensive, and I could've seen me face in 'is boots 'ad I been closer."

Anthony's mind was racing. Two men, not one, and the second no common thief.

"Which of them attacked me? Did you see?"

Codder was regretful.

"No, we didn't, fer when we saw the pair 'o 'em, we ducked down, so as we shouldn't be caught. We 'eard you fall and popped up agin, but Mortimer, the clumsy oaf, knocked over a bucket."

"I couldn't 'elp it: didn't see it there. 'Ere, m'lord, can't we git away from this place. Fair gives me the creeps."

"In a moment, Master Smythe. Was there anything else, Codder?"

Horace scratched his head.

"Not much. We 'eard a chinkin' sound, and then footsteps runnin'. After that, there was an 'orse, galloping away very fast."

"You heard one of the men drop the money-bag and run; the other ride away?"

"That's about the size of it."

"Well, they'll try again." Dunmorrow picked up the lantern. "Since you had the sense to retrieve the gold, they'll make another move, but I'll be ready for them next time. Now, we'd better make a proper search inside, so we are quite certain that Sir Christmas isn't here."

Smythe squawked, and got a clout across the ear from Horace for his pains, but even Codder was reluctant to enter Cheshire House.

"Don't like the look o' it, m'lord."

"Then stay here, and I'll go alone."

That was too much of a challenge for Horace's pride and, dragging the protesting Smythe after him, he followed Dunmorrow inside.

They went into every room, boards creaking as if about to give way under them; Mortimer clutching Codder's arm when the light shewed up the beady bright eyes of the rats which had made their home there.

"Well, that's that." Anthony brushed the dirt off his coat. "Not a damned thing, and no sign of Dee. And why did they want me to come here, if not to exchange Sir Christmas for the money?"

"If I was them," said Codder candidly, "I wouldn't 'ave chosen the actual place I'd got me prisoner."

"Why not?"

"Well, simple, ain't it? Yer could 'ave got Sir ... 'ere ... is 'is name really Christmas?"

"Yes, yes." The earl was impatient. "I could have got Dee, and what?"

"Attacked me and got the money back. Better to git the gold first, and then tells yer some other place ter go and look fer Sir Christmas."

"But it was I who was attacked, not the other way round. Perhaps one of these men simply lured me here to rob me, having no intention of revealing the whereabouts of Dee."

"But 'e'd 'ave ter know 'e was missin', wouldn't 'e?" Codder was pensive. "That's fer certain, otherwise 'e couldn't 'ave writted that note."

"That's true. Maybe it was the second man who came to make the bargain, and the one who struck me down was privy to Dee's disappearance. I don't like it."

"Neither do I," replied Horace fervently. "Two of 'em at it; no, I don't likes it at all. Can we go 'ome now?"

"I suppose so. There's no point in hanging about here. Both the men have gone, whoever they were. Where's your horse?"

The earl, whose head was aching violently, let out a string of ripe imprecations when he found that the mare which Codder had purloined from the stables at Ardley had gone lame.

"Yer lordship could go on ahead," suggested Codder hopefully. "Me and Mortimer 'ud follow yer."

"The Devil you would! You'd be off in a trice, and I haven't finished with you yet. Walk in front of me, and remember, I'm not a patient man, nor a believer in the sanctity of human life."

When they finally reached Ardley, Dunmorrow discovered that his father, far from retiring for the night, had roused three servants and was practising archery in the wide corridor which led to the music-room.

"Oh God," said the earl in the tone of one driven to his limit. "Does he never go to sleep?"

The footmen were thinking much the same thing. Each was holding a lantern to light the target, convinced that the next arrow would find its way to his heart.

"Your money, sir." said Anthony and laid it on a table by the wall. "I didn't require it after all."

The marquis let fly a quarrel which met its mark with deadly accuracy.

"Money?" He lowered his bow. "Thank you, my boy. Shews a touchin' streak of affection in you to give your father such a gift; very touchin'."

"It is yours." The earl held on to his self-control with great difficulty. "If you recall, I borrowed it from you an hour or so ago."

"Did you?" Another arrow was put into place. "Well, fancy that. Hey, steady with that light down there. Do you want to go to your graves to-night, you blockheads?"

"Father! These men are tired, and in a short time they'll have to start work again. For pity's sake, stop this."

Ashbourne put his bow down.

"Hadn't thought of that. Yes, perhaps you're right. Here, take this."

He beckoned the flunkeys to him and reluctantly they drew nearer. No wonder people called this man the Mad Marquis. They had thought Dee bad enough, but his noble guest was beyond belief.

He never seemed to rest and his pastimes left them bereft of speech. Only that morning, the marquis had been slashing the air with his rapier, and it wasn't until he'd left the dining-room that Rourke and Jenkins realised that his lordship had nearly sliced the tops off all the candles on the table, leaving each severed portion exactly in its previous place. Then there was the occasion when he had challenged two of the younger stable-hands to a contest of bending iron bars. The bet was a good one, and Fosset and Bates were strapping men with bulging muscles. Their confident smiles had faded into consternation when the marquis's thin, well-cared-for hands had doubled up the bar as if it were made of wax.

They prayed he wasn't going to suggest some new game,

their faces covered with the sweat of fear, their eyes dulled with fatigue.

Ashbourne emptied the money-bag into their hands, as if the coins were no more than sweetmeats, and they were too overcome to offer thanks for the fortune which they were holding.

"Well, m'boy," said the marquis. "Time you were in bed. Bad habit, staying up as late as this. Should take an example from me."

He smiled with sweet benevolence, and took himself off, leaving the earl dumbstruck.

Finally, Anthony managed to rouse himself before he dropped in his tracks. The servants had disappeared and inside his skull a hundred hammers were banging away. He spent the minimum of time explaining to Elliot what had happened, and then fell across his bed. He didn't even bother to undress: he would have to be up in a couple of hours to start again. But that was two hours away; just then, he was too tired to care.

*   *   *

When Anthony aroused, after what seemed a mere ten minutes, he changed his clothes, got a fresh mount and set off for Brighton to see Sir Christopher Blackstone.

Blackstone was sporting a waistcoat of silver and purple, looking rather pleased with himself as he offered Anthony a glass of Madeira.

"Got good news for me, have you?" he enquired, sipping his own wine. "Want to get this thing settled as soon as possible. Any sign of Dee yet?"

"No, and all the news I have for you is bad. As for wishing to settle matters, no one desires that more than I."

Quickly he related his experiences of the previous night, omitting any reference to Codder and Smythe. Apart from the fact that he had given his word not to mention their existence to anyone, his conviction that they weren't responsible for the attack on him had hardened. If it had been they who had struck him down, they would have run off with the gold.

"Mm." Blackstone was thoughtful. "Who knew that you were going to Cheshire House?"

"Sir Elliot, and my father. I forgot to tell you that the marquis arrived at Ardley after your visit, although his reason for doing so is still obscure, at least to me. I didn't explain to him why I was going; I let him believe it was a hell where I proposed to gamble, but he was busy playing bowls at the time. I don't think he was paying much attention. But I'm sure that I was overheard when I was speaking to him about the money I needed."

"Oh? What makes you think that?"

"I'm certain that there was a sound. I looked round at once, but there wasn't anyone about as far as I could see, yet I sensed strongly that someone had been listening."

"Why didn't you take Elliot Dalzell with you?" Sir Christopher picked up a snuff-box covered with tiny emeralds, gazing at it fondly. "I suggested that he should help you."

"He wanted to come, of course, but the letter said I had to go alone."

"Ah yes, the letter. Funny thing, that."

"I didn't think so last night, particularly when my head was nearly cracked open."

"No, no, of course not. You must be more careful. There may be other attempts on your life. Most encouraging."

Dunmorrow, who still felt far from his best, said shortly:

"I'm glad you think so, sir."

"Anthony, I'm not unsympathetic, but don't you see? You must be getting warm. Wonder why the man ran off without the money."

The earl's annoyance had subsided. He could hardly tell Blackstone why, or that there had been two men, not one, unless he mentioned Horace and Mortimer.

"Perhaps he was disturbed. In any event, Dee wasn't in the house."

"No, but whoever wrote to you won't let it rest at that. He'll try again, whatever his game is."

"A pleasing prospect."

The speculative eyes examined the earl's face for a moment or two.

"Want to give up and go back to London?"

"Certainly not. I'm damned if I'll have some cut-throat attack me and suffer no retribution. Besides, I rather liked old Dee. It's monstrous that a mild, inoffensive man like that should have been abducted and held to ransom."

"Quite." One podgy finger was stroking the small box, Sir Christopher's lids dropping to conceal his expression. "As you say, quite monstrous. By the way, how is your good father?"

"In my view, sir, as mad as a March hare."

Blackstone replaced the snuff-box on the desk and smiled.

"Don't you believe it, m'dear Dunmorrow. Nothing wrong with Ashbourne's brain-box."

"If you were a fellow guest, I think you might have cause to change your mind. When I returned to Ardley it was nearly dawn, yet the marquis was playing with bows and arrows, instead of sleeping in his bed where he should have been."

Blackstone gave a guffaw.

"Got to admit he's got style. Did he hit the target?"

"Of course."

"Yes, as you say, of course. He always does. Take care, Anthony. Don't want anything to happen to you. Watch your step."

"Be assured that I will," – the earl rose – "although I consider myself in less danger from those responsible for taking Sir Christmas than from my own father. Don't be surprised if you learn that I've been impaled by an arrow, or rendered senseless by one of his lordship's bowls."

"Nothing surprises me. Give my regards to Ashbourne."

"With pleasure, but I doubt if he'll remember who you are. He seems to have great difficulty in recalling who I am, never mind anyone else."

When Dunmorrow had gone, Blackstone poured himself another glass of Madeira, drumming his fingers on his desk. Things were beginning to move, and it shouldn't be too long now before whoever had Dee shewed his hand once more.

There was something about the earl's tale of the night before which he didn't quite understand. Blackstone was an expert at reading between the lines and assessing words which hadn't been spoken. What was it that the earl had seen, which had made him hesitate a second too long when relating the story?

After a while he pushed the matter aside. Dee wasn't his only problem and reluctantly he pulled a sheaf of papers towards him and got on with his daily labours.

* * *

"I keep trying to talk to the earl about us." Imelda gave a sob into her damp handkerchief. "He just won't listen to me. He says he's too busy, although what he has to do, I simply can't imagine. I think he only says that, so that he won't have to hear the truth. Peter, I'm sure he means to go ahead and marry me."

"Dearest." Guildford held her hands in his. "Don't distress yourself like this, for I cannot bear to see you so sad. And you won't have to wed him, I promise you."

"You mean it? Oh, do say you mean it!"

Guildford felt strength surge into him as the large mournful eyes implored him for confirmation. He wasn't the same man since he'd met Imelda. He didn't know how or why he had changed; he was just sure that he had. Instead of keeping to heel at Davina's command, he was now the strong one, his confidence growing with each day that passed.

"Of course I mean it. Soon, I shall tell him myself. He does strike me as being preoccupied, although, like you, I can't think why. It is so quiet and peaceful here, except that Sir Christmas hasn't come back, and, of course, because of the marquis."

"You don't think Anthony is worried because of Sir Christmas, do you? Surely nothing could really have happened to him."

"No, I'm sure it hasn't. He often goes away for a day or two; his servants have said so. No, if the earl is distrait, it is more likely to be because of his father. Why, only just now I saw him running a race with three of the coachmen. What a good thing it is that you're not going to marry into such a family! After all, one never knows whether such things are hereditary."

"No, but Anthony has never run races, as far as I know."

"There is always time. Darling, your lips are so tempting that I fear I shall be forced to kiss them."

"Peter!"

She tried to be shocked, but when he drew her nearer to him she was as eager as he to taste the first fruits of their love. She was pink and confused when he released her, but he saw the wonder in her and was content.

"I have written a poem about you."

"About me? But I am nothing."

"You are everything, my sweet. Will you hear my poor offering?"

"I cannot wait. Every word will be a precious jewel to me."

Guildford sighed. It was exactly as it should be. Imelda would be an enthralled listener, unlike Davina who had endured his verse with the long-suffering air of a patient nanny.

He took the sheet of paper from his pocket.

"Well, here it is. I pray that you will favour it."

"I know I will. Dear Peter; I do love you so."

* * *

Whilst Imelda Russell and Guildford were enjoying raptuous moments in the garden, the marquis and Lady Rosamond were playing cards in the library.

"Well," said Ashbourne, "I may not have seen you for ten years or so, but you haven't changed a whit. As desirable as ever you were, Louisa."

"I am not Louisa!" Rosamond was incensed. "Don't be so provoking. You know quite well who I am, and we met not six months ago. Do stop wool-gathering, and pay attention to your hand."

"Not Louisa?" He looked vague. "Well I never! Could have sworn you were the Sheldon girl."

"I'm not a girl, nor am I Matthew Sheldon's daughter. Now, what cards have you got?"

To her chagrin, the marquis had the winning hand. Indeed, since they had started playing some hour before, the marquis had won every single game. Rosamond looked at him accusingly. There were times when one was forced to consider whether Ashbourne was as much of a fool as he appeared to be.

"What's your brother going to say when he learns Davina isn't going to marry Guildford?" Ashbourne was shuffling the cards. "Think he'll mind very much?"

"He will celebrate by getting roaring drunk, or visiting that village whore of his, and begetting another bastard."

"The admirable Bessie."

"How did you know about her?" Lady Rosamond was startled. It seemed that there was nothing of which the marquis was not aware, however small and insignificant the subject. "I can't imagine how you could have heard about that strumpet."

"It's hardly a secret, is it?" The marquis was dealing quickly and with a very professional touch. "Don't be too hard on Gervase, m'dear. He was lonely."

"Poppycock! And I am forced to tell you that you deal as if you were one of those dreadful persons in a gambling-hole."

"Hell. Gambling-hell."

"Don't quibble. Are you sure you're not cheating?"

"Quite." Ashbourne was studying his new cards. "I would, of course, if it were necessary, but it ain't. Lucky enough, without recourse to sleight of hand."

"You are impossible!"

When she could see he wasn't listening, she returned to his earlier question.

"Why did you ask whether Gervase would mind if Davina didn't marry Guildford?"

"Because it's perfectly plain that she's not going to. Your play."

"She has plighted her troth to him."

The marquis threw down an ace.

"What an absurd phrase that is! Always sounds indecent to me."

"How can you say such things? It's exactly the opposite. It means ..."

"I know what it means." He was musing over his next move. "But whatever she has done with her troth, Louisa, she won't marry Peter Guildford. You know that as well as I do. Well, what have you got?"

"A headache," she snapped. "How do you expect me to concentrate when you keep talking such rubbish?"

He glanced up and grinned.

"Worried about her, aren't you? Can see she's in love, and not with young Peter. What are you going to do about it?"

"Me?" She had flushed, put out because he was always so perceptive. "I shall do nothing at all. It's not my business."

"Then I suppose it will be left to me. Ah well; it won't be the first time."

"It's nothing to do with you either, and I would advise you not to meddle."

"It has everything to do with me."

She felt herself melting under his smile. Ashbourne could be quite infuriating. She had wanted to remain enraged with him, but it was extremely hard to do.

"I can't see how."

She was no longer acid, pretending not to notice that he had laid one hand over hers.

"Question of who will carry on my line. Very important. Blood is everything."

She stared at him uncomprehendingly.

"Line? Blood? Francis, whatever are you talking about?"

"Don't worry your pretty head about it, and since you have no notion how to play this game let us go for a walk. I know one or two parts of the grounds where one can't be seen from the house."

She drew herself up, ready to put him firmly in his place, only to find herself being led, unresisting, to the door.

"That's right. Leave everything to me, Louisa; I know what to do." His hand tightened on her arm. "Now, shall it be the arbour, or the copse at the far side of the fountain? Doesn't really matter for what we have in mind, does it? One spot is as good as another."

* * *

For most of the morning Davina had lectured herself about keeping a still tongue, and not interfering with things which weren't her business.

She sat on a rustic bench, by herself as usual, aware that Imelda and Peter had gone off together, and that the marquis and Rosamond, for some unaccountable reason, had just crossed the lawn and disappeared behind a copse some way away. It was rather like being marooned on an island, and when the earl appeared she steeled herself to indulge in light repartee, and not to ask questions which would involve her in another quarrel with him.

"Alone again?" His tone was like the prick of a needle. "What can the men in this house be thinking of, and where is your lover?"

She set her teeth, still determined to remain aloof.

"I don't know what is the matter with the men in this house, sir, including you, and if by my lover you mean Peter, he is somewhere in the grounds with Imelda."

"Yes, of course. Where else would he be?" I would have come to keep you company before this, but I had to ride to Brighton early to-day."

"You seem to do a lot of riding." Her firm resolution was slipping away. "Not only early this morning, but also in the middle of the night."

His half-smiled vanished.

"Madam?"

"I couldn't sleep." She faced him boldly. "I was looking out of the window and saw you go. It was very late. I should have been in bed, but ..."

"... you couldn't sleep. Beautiful women shouldn't waste their time in bed, sleeping." He was caustic. "Few women of my acquaintance do." He was cursing to himself because she had seen him, and before long would start asking questions which he didn't want to answer. The only recourse was to make her so angry that she would go away in a huff. "What a pity I was otherwise engaged, or I could have filled your waking hours much more satisfactorily. Gazing out of a window is so dull."

"How dare you! I've a good mind to speak to the marquis."

"I wouldn't if I were you," he advised coolly, wishing he could take her in his arms there and then. "It might put ideas into his head."

"You are intolerable!"

After a moment or two, she said slowly:

"I think you're merely being outrageous to hide from me

the real reason for your excursion. Are you going to tell me what you were doing?"

"No." He was imperturbable on the surface, and extremely worried beneath it. "I am not. It is none of your business and, in any event, you wouldn't like the truth."

"I see." She sat up straighter. "No, perhaps you are right. The name of your mistress is not my concern."

He wanted flatly to deny that he had gone to visit a woman, but it was one way out of a difficult situation. It would hurt Davina, until he was free to tell her the truth, but at least she wouldn't get mixed up with whatever was going on. If she once learned of the task set him by Blackstone, she would insist on helping him, for that was the kind of girl she was.

"Do you deny it?"

"What?"

It struck him that of late he was becoming very inattentive, his mind drifting off into other things in the middle of a conversation. He put it down to the fact that he was staying in the same house as his father. Almost anyone's mind would wander in such circumstances, and he wished Davina wouldn't look at him like that, because the desire he felt for her was practically impossible to control.

"I said, do you deny it?"

"I have had mistresses." He was evasive and offhand. "Most men do, if they have half a chance."

Her eyes were quite wonderful when she was furious, and she was furious now.

"How like you to bring Bessie into this!"

"Bessie?"

He stove gamely to marshal his scattered thoughts: clearly, he had missed yet another point by mooning over Davina's loveliness.

"Yes, Bessie Lowe. It is unforgiveable of you to mention her."

He considered the possibility that he might be suffering from a slight concussion: the blow on the head had been a hard one. If it were not that, then he was becoming as addle-pated as the marquis.

"Pray forgive me," he said at last, realising it was beyond him to work out the mystery of Bessie Lowe. "I don't know who this woman is you're talking about, and I feel sure I didn't mention her name, but if I have unwittingly offended you I apologise."

She glared at him.

"You didn't mention her name; you are far too subtle for that. But I knew whom you meant. Because I have had to endure her for so many years, it does not mean I have to have her thrust down my throat whilst I am here."

She got up, twitching her skirt away, as if he were contaminated.

"Good-day, sir."

"There isn't much use in bidding me farewell and leaving me in high dudgeon. We shall be having luncheon together in some fifteen minutes' time."

"The sooner the Regent pays his promised visit, and I can return to Hillborough Hall, the better I shall be pleased. Then I shall not have to inconvenience myself by avoiding you."

"If that's how you feel about me, you can't begrudge me my mistress," he said airily. "Come; be fair. You can't have it both ways."

He saw the brightness of her eyes and realised that tears weren't far off.

"Don't," he said in quite a different tone of voice. "Davina, don't cry over me, I don't deserve it."

"That is the first word of truth you have spoken this morning, my lord, and now please let me go. I shall have a tray sent up to my room."

He sighed as she almost ran across the grass to get away from him. He felt giddy again, not sure whether it was his recent injury or the sight of Davina's slender but sensuous figure under the flimsy muslin gown. He ought to have given her a good shaking, and then held her tightly to him, but the time wasn't ripe.

Better that she should think he had been dallying with a whore, than mixed up with unscrupulous men. Nothing must endanger her life; he loved her far too much for that.

Seven

It was that same afternoon that Davina Temple made the decision to look for Christmas Dee.

Apart from the fact that she had liked him, she had to know the truth about his disappearance. Time was passing, and the fact that he hadn't returned home was of increasing concern to her, because it strengthened her suspicions of the Earl of Dunmorrow.

Believing the man she loved might be capable of murder was a bitter pill to swallow, but Davina was not a girl to blench from unpleasantness.

It was true that there could be other reasons for Dee's continuing absence; it might even be that Anthony was in no way involved. Yet small things added up to a very frightening whole. The earl had admitted to being in Ireland at the time when the man mentioned in Mirabel's letter had been killed; he had needed a thousand guineas in a hurry, and had ridden off into the night. When Gunn had been found dead, by some miracle the Regent's representatives had arrived to smooth away the anxieties of the guests, and then the Marquis of Ashbourne had appeared.

There was only one thing to do, and that was to try to find out what had happened to her host. She cast an eye round the assembled guests as they gathered for tea. None of them seemed in the least worried by the fact that Dee was still missing, accepting like so many sheep the words of assurance offered by Sir Christopher Blackstone.

However, in fairness to them, and Davina always tried to be fair, she hadn't taken any steps to find Dee either. She had been too busy quarrelling with the earl, and falling in love with him, but this omission must now be remedied. If she could discover what had become of Sir Christmas, she would know whether or not her doubts about Dunmorrow were justified.

She tried not to dwell upon the possibility that her first assumption was correct as she planned her campaign. It seemed sensible to look round Ardley before doing anything else. There were many places in the house, and outside, where a body could have been hidden. Blackstone's men had only removed one corpse, the luckless Robert's, so if Dee had met his end at Ardley he was still there.

With her normal efficiency she worked out the most logical place to start: the basements. They would be deserted at night, but they probably contained any number of storerooms, closets and cupboards.

There would be no interruption from the servants, for they were all scared sick by the ghost they imagined they had seen, and wouldn't go downstairs in the dark. The problem would be Hortensia Moffat, who slept as lightly as a cat, ready to pounce at the slightest noise.

Fortunately, Aunt Rosamond was prone to slumber very soundly, and would be no trouble, but Horty had to be dealt with.

Davina hovered in the corridor outside her room until Alice brought the hot chocolate. It wasn't normal for one's maid to be included in such bed-time luxury, but Horty wasn't a normal maid, and for once Davina was profoundly thankful for it.

She took the tray from Alice, smiling her thanks, waiting for the girl to trot off down the stairs. The small phial of laudanum, which Aunt Rosamond carried in case of her imaginary ear-ache, had been surreptitiously removed earlier in the day. Davina added some drops to Horty's cup, praying it wasn't a lethal dose, and then sat down to wait for the servants to retire.

Her thoughts during that time were not pleasant companions. She wasn't in the least afraid of her proposed search of the basements, nor of the possibility of meeting wandering spirits. What tore at her, until she could have cried, was the fact that Anthony might be guilty.

It was after midnight when she left her room, having checked that Rosamond and Horty, who had a truckle-bed in the former's chamber for convenience sake, were fast asleep.

She had had the forethought to take a lantern from one of the stables that afternoon, realising that a candle in a draughty passage below ground would not be of much use.

She went down the main stairs and into the kitchen. It wasn't likely that Dee would be there, but she was determined to miss nothing. She moved on to the larder, to the cold-room where butter and milk were kept and then into a large room where the maids did the laundry. The presses were full of clean linen, but of Dee there was no trace. With a sigh she walked along to the other end of the corridor.

It seemed chillier there, and soon she came upon the steps down which Robert Gunn had fallen, or had been pushed. For a second she could see the sightless eyes and his awkward, twisted limbs; then she shut the picture firmly out of her mind and turned the corner, opening the door to the first store-room. It contained nothing but rubbish and a few pieces of broken furniture, but not a single nook or cranny where a cadaver could be concealed.

She was just backing out of the store, prepared to inspect the next one, when a rough hand clamped itself over her mouth and she found herself dragged bodily inside a small, stinking hovel.

She struggled furiously, finally freeing herself, turning in outrage to face her molester. She thought she had never seen a man so tall and so thin, and immediately realised why the servants imagined they had seen a spectre. The man looked as if he were a skeleton, and his squarish, unshaven face was formidable.

Nevertheless, Davina's courage didn't flag, mostly because she was so angry that the dirty, bedraggled creature had had the temerity to touch her. Furthermore, she knew that in such confrontations the secret was to overawe one's opponent, before one's own spirit was sapped.

"How dare you?" The hazel eyes were as flinty as steel. "Who are you, and what are you doing here?"

To say that Horace was taken aback by her reaction was an understatement. He had grown so used to people cowering away from him, particularly slips of girls like this one, that his mouth dropped open, temporarily struck dumb.

"Well?" Davina had picked up her lantern, holding it high so that she could see her attacker the better, noticing a small fat man, crouched on the ground, looking extremely nervous. "Who are you?"

"Keep quiet, yer bitch." Codder had managed to regain his self-confidence. "Another word, and I'll cut yer throat."

Without a second's hesitation Davina flung open the door again and backed two steps out into the corridor.

"My maid is waiting at the end of the main passage," she said firmly and quite untruthfully. "One scream from me, and the whole household will be down here in seconds."

Codder gaped. He had never met a woman like this before and he wasn't quite sure what to do about her. Tentatively, he drew his knife, thrusting it back jerkily as Davina opened her mouth wide, as if to shout the place down.

"Orl right, yer needn't yell out," he growled. "Come in 'ere though, so's we can talk."

"Don't be a fool." Davina was scornful. "I'm not coming an inch nearer to you, for you smell like a cess-pit. I give you one moment to explain who you are, and then I shall scream, and, sir, be assured that my scream is quite ear-splitting."

Codder didn't doubt if for a second, his hands hanging limply at his side. First the dandy with the pistol, and now this virago. Was ever a man as unlucky as he?

"Me name's Codder, and this 'ere is Smythe: Mortimer Smythe."

He looked helplessly at Mortimer, who was almost transfixed by what was taking place in front of him.

"Well, go on." Davina was tapping her foot. "So those are your names, but who are you, and what are you doing here? Remember, when I scream ..."

"Yes, yes," Codder said hastily. "I was goin' ter tell yer."

"Then get on with it."

She listened to Horace's tale of woe; the escape from prison and the discovery of the trap-door; the thankfulness the pair of them had felt when they had found the seldom-used store.

"And I suppose the servants came upon you, and you forced them to keep quiet, is that it? You made them give you food, and threatened them with that knife, if they gave you away."

"Well, we was 'ungry."

"You are despicable! Those girls were beside themselves with fear. At first, they thought you were a ghost, although in the end they probably wished you had been, for then, at least, you could have been exorcised."

"Eh?"

"Never mind." She hesitated, then decided to plung in. "Do you know whose house this is?"

"We didn't at first, not till 'is 'igh and mightiness found us, and told us."

For the first time Davina felt a shiver inside herself.

"His high and mightiness? Who is that?"

"Can't tells yer that, even if I knew. Gave me word I

wouldn't. 'Sides, 'e said 'e'd cut me ears orf and feed them to the pigs if I told anyone 'e'd bin 'ere.''

She let out her breath gently

"I see. You don't have to tell me; I'll tell you. That was the Earl of Dunmorrow.''

Smythe choked, and Codder said quickly:

"I didn't say nothin'. I kept me word. You'll tell 'im that, won't you?''

"No, not unless you answer my questions honestly, if it is in you to be honest.''

"We'll tells yer anythin', only fer Gawd's sake don't let 'im know you've spoken to us, or 'e'll never believe you guessed. 'E'll 'ave me 'ears, and ...''

"Do be quiet!'' Davina's mouth was a straight line, and any one of her father's servants would have recognised the mood she was in. "I am not interested in your ears, and I doubt if the pigs would be either. They're very clean animals, you know. What was the earl doing here?''

It was Codder's turn to make a decision, and he did it without a qualm. True, the earl hadn't betrayed them, yet, on the other hand, but for his and Mortimer's following his lordship to Cheshire House, the latter might be dead and buried by now. A favour for a favour.

"Well, miss, I'll tells yer, if yer gives yer word to keep it a secret between us.''

Davina had no desire to be hampered with such a promise, but as the men were so afraid of Dunmorrow, she'd get no sense out of them unless she agreed.

"Very well.'' She gave her acquiescence reluctantly. "I promise I won't tell the earl, or anybody else about you, if you will explain what his lordship was doing here, and what he said to you.''

"No one at all, miss?''

"No! Don't waste my time.''

"Well, 'e said 'e'd not tell about us, if we 'elped 'im.''

"To do what?''

Horace's eyes were watering with the effort of keeping his lies plausible enough to convince this friend, whose exquisite lips might open at any moment and create total havoc for him and Mortimer.

"It were ter do with a man with a funny name."

Davina's expression didn't alter. She wasn't going to let these two scoundrels know how near she was to breaking down.

"Sir Christmas Dee?"

"That's the one."

"How were you to help him? What did he want you to do?"

Codder felt easier. The girl seemed to believe him, and she didn't look quite so fierce as she had a moment or two ago. Simply telling her that the earl had wanted him to question the servants was too tame; best to scare the living daylights out of her, and make her as afraid of the earl as he was.

"We don't know yet, miss. 'E's comin' back ter tell us, but we don't know when. Move a body, like as not. That's what it seemed ter me."

Davina swallowed hard. It was what she had feared of all along, but confirmation was as agonizing as having a dagger stuck through one.

"I see."

"What'll yer do?"

She was mistress of herself once more.

"Nothing for the present. I have given you my word that I won't tell anyone that I've seen you; you must give me the same assurance. No one must know I've been here. Is that understood?"

"'Course it is!" Horace was fervent. He was only too happy to agree; the last thing he wanted was for the earl to start questioning this little madam. "We gives our word."

"For what that's worth," she returned shortly. "And soon I shall come back, and you will tell me what service the earl wishes you to render him.''

''Eh?''

''For heaven's sake! You'll tell me what he wants you to do, particularly if it concerns a body, as you think it may do. I'm going now. If you have any ideas about following me into the passage, I would advise you to dismiss them. As I have told you, my maid is along there. You would be back in prison before you could count to ten: if you can count.''

When she had gone, Mortimer said weakly:

''Never met one like 'er before, Horace, 'ave you?''

''No, nor does I want to meet another, bloody young 'arpy.''

''Still, I don't thinks yer should 'ave let 'er believe the earl was the one what did away with Sir Christmas, or whatever e's called. Now she thinks 'im guilty, and 'e ain't done us no 'arm.''

''Ain't done us much good neither.''

''Fancy 'im bein' an earl, and 'e didn't give us away.''

''We've paid fer that. Now stop worryin' about 'is lordship, and worry about yerself. If that brazen 'ussy ever gits ter talkin' ter the earl, you and me will be where 'e said we'd be: buried in the yard at Stockland. Let's 'ope I've scared 'er enough to keep 'em apart. Now 'and me that bottle. I've 'ad more 'un I can stand fer one night.''

* * *

The following morning Davina asked Sir Elliot Dalzell if he would accompany her for a walk in the garden.

She had spent the night pondering on her next move and had decided that she needed help and advice. Having reached that conclusion, the more difficult matter of whom to trust had to be settled. She could trust Peter, of course, but he would be quite useless in such a situation.

She didn't really see Stuart Barminster as a cold-blooded ally of the earl's, but she didn't like him either. Sir Percy she dismissed without a second thought, along with Aunt

Rosamond, Horty and Lady Jessica. All of them would be quite hopeless in their various ways, and the marquis wasn't impartial.

That left Sir Elliot. Since he was a friend of the earl's, if there was any chance of proving Dunmorrow's innocence Dalzell would be the man to do it, and she desperately wanted Anthony to be innocent.

Elliot was somewhat surprised, for Davina Temple had shewn no previous inclination to converse with him alone, but he was never averse to talking to a pretty woman and he led her to a small arbour some way from the house, seating her on the rustic bench which was placed in front of thick laurel-bushes.

"I don't quite know how to begin, Sir Elliot." Davina was making quite a to-do of adjusting her York tan gloves. "It is so awkward, particularly as he is your friend."

Elliot smiled. The reason for the tête-à-tête was now apparent. Davina was in love with Anthony and wanted to know how the earl felt, and whether he was prepared to forego matrimony with Imelda Russell.

'I'm a good listener," he said encouragingly. "What about Anthony?"

When she started her tale his smile faded abruptly, and by the time she had concluded he appeared to have lost the power of speech.

"Anthony," he said at last. "A murderer? Lady Davina, you must be mistaken. He would never do such things."

"I pray that you're right; I do so much want you to be, and I knew you'd say that, being a loyal person. But the evidence does mount up, doesn't it? And there's the letter which my friend's aunt wrote to Sir Christmas, mentioning a name, and now Miss Southey has written similarly to me."

"A name?"

"Yes. I'm sure it's an alias, but it wouldn't be difficult to discover the man's real identity, would it? I mean, to confirm that it was actually the earl using a false name."

Dalzell's mouth was hard, and it seemed to Davina a long time before he spoke.

"No, it could be done. As you say, it wouldn't be too difficult. Is there anything else?"

"I don't think so." Davina hadn't mentioned the felons, for she had promised not to, and in any event there seemed to her to be enough black marks against Dunmorrow without bringing them into it at that stage. "I believe I've covered everything. I told you that he was the son of a marquis, didn't I?"

Dalzell nodded.

"Yes you did; you have been most succinct. You must forgive me if I appeared unresponsive at first, but this has been a dire revelation."

"I realise that, and I'm sorry to burden you with the story, but I had to confide in someone. If I have totally misunderstood the situation, and no one hopes that this is so more than I do, you'd want to establish the truth, wouldn't you?"

"Certainly." He was very sober. "Yes, naturally I would. Since it is clear that you have some feeling for the earl, it is very brave of you to have told me all this."

"It's not a question of feeling." She refused to admit to Dalzell that her interest was anything but altruistic. "It is simply a matter of getting at the truth."

"Of course. Now, Lady Davina, it is essential that you have nothing more to do with this. It isn't safe for you to be mixed up in such an affair. You'd better give me the letter you received from your friend. Have you got it with you?"

"No, it's in my room."

"Then give it to me at luncheon."

"Very well. What will you do?"

"I'm not sure yet; I shall have to think about it. Have you told anyone, anyone at all, that you were going to speak to me?"

"No, no one else knows of my fears."

"Then please don't mention this talk to a soul, no matter

how much you feel you can trust them. Leave the whole thing in my hands."

"Very well, but ..."

"Please promise me your silence. It could jeopardize my own life if you give even a hint of it. You can see the danger, can't you? Christmas Dee had a letter from your friend's aunt, and now ..."

She gripped her hands tighter together.

"Yes, of course. I shall say nothing. You think that Sir Christmas is dead, don't you?"

"It is a possibility."

"And Robert Gunn."

"We mustn't guess. Please do as I ask you; put it all out of your mind. Now, I think it would be better if you returned to the house alone. It might not be wise for us to be seen together, except in company."

She thanked Elliot and made her way back, leaving Dalzell to take a different route across the grounds.

There was quietness for a moment or two; then the laurel-bushes rustled for a few seconds before falling still again, leaving the arbour silent and peaceful once more.

* * *

When Hortensia Moffat shewed the Marquis of Ashbourne into Lady Rosamond's room, the latter threw up her hands in despair.

"No! Absolutely not! I simply haven't got time to play games with you now. I'm dressing for luncheon. All right, Horty, you may go."

"No games," said Ashbourne cheerfully as the door closed behind a piqued Hortensia. "I want you to get a letter from your niece's room for me, Louisa. She's not there. I've just left her downstairs talking to Peter Guildford, although goodness knows why she's doing that."

"Because she is to marry him." Rosamond was goaded beyond endurance. "And I've told you a hundred times or more that I'm not Louisa. Furthermore, I've no intention of taking anything from Davina's room. What next?"

The marquis pursed his lips.

"Don't really know what's next. Only know that the gel would be safer without it. Get it for me, and hurry."

"How do you know she's got a letter, and which one do you mean?"

"Has she had so many since she's been here? Come, don't dilly-dally. The one I want is from a woman in Ireland. Heard Davina mention it to someone."

"You shouldn't have been eavesdropping." Rosamond was severe. "What do you want it for, anyway?"

"I've just told you; she'll be much better off without it. Do this for me, Louisa, and I'll shew you how to use the foils."

Irritated, Lady Rosamond turned from the mirror to face the marquis, her lips parting to express her opinion of a man who couldn't remember people's names, and who wanted others to steal for him.

Then her eyes met his and, had a pin chose to fall on the carpet at that moment, it would have sounded like the knell of doom.

Rosamond rose from the dressing-table, her arguments done, shaken by what she'd seen in Ashbourne.

"Very well; wait here. I'll get it for you."

"Thank you, my dear." He patted her cheek as she handed him the letter. "Don't tell anyone about this, will you?"

He saw the questioning look but killed it at birth.

"No one at all. If the matter's mentioned, you don't know what's happened to the damned thing. Good girl, Louisa. We'll go riding to-morrow, shall we?"

Rosamond drew in a deep breath, ready to remind Ashbourne yet again that her baptismal name was not Louisa, but suddenly found herself saying happily:

"Why yes, Francis, I should like that very much.

"And I."

Her pleasure faded and she began to look worried.

"There's nothing wrong with Davina, is there? She's not in any sort of danger?"

The marquis smiled and it seemed to Rosamond that she was being bathed in sunlight.

"No, not any more. Now that I have the letter, she is quite safe. Rest assured, my dear. I have got what I wanted."

Eight

Davina felt a measure of relief after she had unburdened herself to Dalzell. There was a strength and reliability about him which was very reassuring. He would know what to do, and how to do it, and whilst he did not seem the kind of man who would pervert the course of justice, equally he would not condemn a friend unless the case were fully proven.

With that off her mind, Davina changed for luncheon. In spite of the steps she had taken to investigate the goings-on of the earl, and the doubts she harboured about him, she still felt dizzy whenever he looked at her. Suspicions, alas, did not cancel out love and, as was the way with women who had lost their hearts, she wanted to look her best. A cambric high gown, beneath a Spanish robe of apricot-coloured muslin, was her choice, with kid slippers to match. When she had finished arranging her hair to her satisfaction, she opened the drawer where she had put Mirabel Southey's letter.

Davina was an almost excessively tidy girl, as her father knew to his cost, and could always say where every one of her possessions was to be found. There was no chance at all that she had slipped the letter in another place and had forgotten about it. Davina didn't forget anything. However, since Elliot had asked particularly for the missive, she searched the tall-boy and her jewel-case. Then she looked in the trunk which contained the smaller items of her wardrobe, but it wasn't there.

The gong summoned the guests downstairs, and she raised her shoulders helplessly when Dalzell managed to sit next to her at table.

"It's gone," she whispered, "I know exactly where I put it, but it isn't there now. I've looked in other places too, but I can't find it."

Dalzell was drinking wine, his face shewing no sign of his concern.

"What do you think has happened to it, Sir Elliot?"

She saw Dunmorrow looking at her, sure that he had guessed about her approach to Elliot. She tried to eat, but the food wouldn't go down, and when the earl turned to speak to Lady Jessica she said in an undertone:

"Sir Elliot, what do you think?"

"It has been taken."

It was as if she had been douched with cold water, and she glanced round to see if anyone had heard, but Dalzell's tone was low. No one else was paying attention to them and she was emboldened to make a further enquiry.

"I'm not sure what you mean. Who has taken the letter?"

He didn't answer, but of course he didn't have to. Anthony, or someone on his behalf, had got into her room and removed Mirabel's note.

"What shall I do?"

"Nothing." Sir Elliot was offering her some fruit. "I've told you, leave things to me, but it must be found." Then he smiled, raising his voice to a normal pitch. "Do have some of these grapes, Lady Davina; they are quite excellent. Anthony, what about you? An apple, perhaps?"

* * *

Davina went into the garden after luncheon. She wanted to be alone to think, and to escape conversations which might lead her to say unwise things.

She saw Rosamond and the marquis down by the pool, the latter trying to shew her aunt the correct way to hold a rapier, although what use such skills would be to Rosamond, Davina had no idea. She has also seen Peter and Imelda, their heads close together. Sooner or later she would have to have a straight talk with Guildford. It was unlikely that her decision not to marry him would cause him grief; indeed, it would probably bring him the utmost relief.

When she got to the terrace on her way back, she could hear voices in the drawing-room. It was wholly foreign to her nature to listen to words not intended for her ears, but this time she put aside her scruples, for what Lady Jessica was saying to Whittingham was startling in the extreme.

"I know you've got the letter, Percy." For once she was very tart with her beau. "It's no use pretending you've lost it, for I know that to be untrue."

Davina couldn't hear Percy's reply and crept closer, concealing herself behind the curtains, ashamed of her reprehensible behaviour.

"Don't be so stupid, of course it's important. You have it, and you must give it to me. Don't you realise what trouble it could cause?"

"It is as secure with me as with you." Whittingham was not being as obliging as normally he was with his mistress. "Why shouldn't I keep it?"

"Because I want it back, that's why. Now give it to me this instant!"

With very great care, Davina looked round the curtains, heart in mouth. If the two of them should see her, she had no idea what kind of explanation she could give, but, fortunately for her, they were too preoccupied with one another.

"Oh very well!" Whittingham was tetchy. "If you must, you must. Here it is."

Davina saw the folded paper pass from Sir Percy to

Jessica, who quickly tucked it down the bodice of her gown.

"Such a fuss," he said peevishly. "I would have been safe enough with me."

"Don't sulk." She was less strident now that she had got her own way. "You know I don't like you to pout; it quite spoils your looks. Come, give me a smile."

"I don't want to." Percy was obstinate. "Sometimes, Jessica, you treat me as if I were five years old."

"That's because you sometimes behave as if you were. Kiss me, quickly, for the others will be back in a minute, including my husband. Barminster may be tolerant, but even he couldn't countenance us making love in Sir Christmas's drawing-room."

Percy didn't appear very anxious to make love in the drawing-room or anywhere else, and after a minute or two Jessica flounced out leaving Whittingham mumbling to himself about the tiresomeness of women.

Davina's head was in a whirl. The conversation she had just overheard, and the passing of a letter from Percy to Jessica, had opened up new and quite unexpected vistas.

The pair of them had looked very furtive, and the letter must have been vital to both of them, since they had quarrelled about who should keep it.

Davina had been so sure that St. Romer was the man to watch that she hadn't given much thought to any of the other men at Ardley. Perhaps Mirabel's letter, and that of her aunt's to Dee, had referred to Percy Whittingham and not to the earl at all. There were many families of high rank living in Ireland, and Mirabel Southey was notorious for not remembering titles. She had said the son of a marquis, but it could have been someone quite different.

It was at that moment that Whittingham turned and saw Daniva. His face lost its colour, as she, making the best of a terrible situation, crossed the floor to his side.

"Sir Percy." She smiled, pretending not to see his hunted look. "We haven't had much time to talk together, have we?

I believe you know my godmother, the Marchioness of Bladen.''

"Yes ... yes I do.''

Percy was trying to ease the stock round his neck, as if it were strangling him.

"Yes, I thought so. I visited her recently, and she spoke of you.''

Davina did not tell Whittingham what trenchant words her godmother had used, but went on to the question which was of burning interest to her.

"I was discussing horses with Sir Elliot earlier. Come, do sit down.''

"'Er, well ... I ...''

She was the picture of innocence.

"Shall I ask my aunt to join us, if you feel we need someone with us. I thought I saw you and Lady Jessica together as I came up the terrace steps, so I didn't think ...''

"No ... no, of course not." Sir Percy sat down as if his legs had given way under him. "What were you saying?''

"I was telling you about Sir Elliot. He has stables, you know, in Ireland.''

Whittingham looked as if he were about to be sick, and Davina had to think quickly. It wouldn't be enough to ask if he had been there in the past: she needed to know whether he had been in Ireland at the end of last year. She decided that as she was going to tell a lie it might as well be a big one.

"He told me had given a large party last winter; just before or after Christmas, I can't remember which. Were you there by any chance?''

Whittingham was now gazing at her as if she were a coiled snake about to strike him dead.

"Well ... I ... uh ...''

Davina paused in her efforts for a second. She couldn't imagine what Jessica Barminster saw in this man, whose conversation seemed limited to a series of grunts and muffled ejaculations. He was comely enough, but his eyes bulged a trifle and his chin was weak: not at all like the earl's, which was as hard as granite. She forced herself to stop thinking of Anthony, and got on with her job.

"Were you there?" she repeated with admirable restraint. "In Ireland, last winter?"

Sir Percy choked. The wretched woman had guessed. He had always known that the trip he and Jessica had taken to Dublin, whilst Barminster was away on business, had been a mistake. Jessica had pooh-poohed his fears, but he hadn't been convinced. Sooner or later he had known they would be exposed, and Barminster, as Jessica had said, was not a man to be cuckolded in public, however disinterested he was in his wife's private doings.

"I ... no that is ... I ..."

It was no use. He couldn't go on, not with those great hazel eyes fixed rigidly on his. He got up unsteadily, hardly stopping to bow or make his apologies as he fled the room.

Davina was left with mixed feelings. Whittingham hadn't actually admitted he'd been in Omagh, but he had looked very like a criminal when she had asked what was, after all, an apparently innocuous question. It was not beyond the realms of possibility, therefore, that Percy had been in Ireland at the time of the tragedy.

Whittingham didn't look as though he could kill a gnat, but his behaviour a moment or two before had been far from normal, and then there was the episode of the letter.

And since there was some doubt about where Sir Percy had been when the murder had occurred Davina resolved to ask the other men a few questions. It would only be common justice, and the earl deserved that much at least.

It wouldn't be easy interrogating the marquis, so she decided to leave him until the last and start with the most vulnerable of her quarry. Guildford was decidedly vulnerable, and a poor liar to boot. He was probably reading his sonnets to Imelda, but that couldn't be helped. He would have to stop for a while and answer some enquiries. The earl must be given every chance, and Davina left the drawing-room and went in search of Guildford.

* * *

Once again Imelda was tearful as she sat in the summer-house on the west side of the grounds.

"It's no use," she sobbed. "The earl simply will not listen to me. I have tried again and again to talk to him, but he always tells me he is too busy to deal with the arrangements for the wedding, and then walks away. Peter! What am I going to do?"

"Dearest heart." Guildford held her to him as if she were made of spun glass. "I can't bear it when you cry like this. If you cannot make Dunmorrow heed you, then I shall speak to him myself."

Her dark eyes almost drowned him.

"Would you? Oh, you are so brave! I wish I had your courage."

"It is for the man to be brave, my love, and I will be most valorous for your sake."

"And what about Lady Davina?"

Peter wilted at the mention of his fiancée's name, although he did his best to hide it. Words were cheap, but he wasn't looking forward to discussing with the Earl of Dunmorrow his love for Imelda Russell. He cared even less for the thought of trying to explain the situation to Davina.

It wasn't that he imagined Davina was in love with him. Since he had realised what true love was, he could see well enough that Davina's feelings towards him were, at best, a mere fondness. Yet she was pig-headed in the extreme. She had made her decision to marry him, and it was unlikely that she would change her mind. After all, every woman had her pride, and Davina had about three times as much as most females.

"I shall make a clean breast of it before we leave here," he said with more confidence that he felt. "As soon as the

Regent's visit is over, I shall face her with the truth."

The next fifteen minutes were spent happily by the pair of them: Peter the comforter; Imelda the comforted. He was just about to suggest that he should make a sketch of her, when to his dire consternation he saw Davina bearing down upon them. There was no time to run, hide or even pretend that he was not alone with Imelda, and his blood turned to ice-water in his veins as Davina entered their hideaway.

"Lady Imelda." Davina spoke gently and her smile was kind. "I hesitate to interrupt you, but I have a need of Peter's ear for a few minutes."

"Of ... of course ... I ..." Imelda's cheeks were scarlet. "I do hope that you will not misconstrue ... that is ... well ... Sir Peter was just reading some poetry to me, but you must be shaken to find that we are not chaperoned."

Davina glanced at Peter. He looked like a fish which had been deprived of water for too long, his embarrassment making him squirm. She paused long enough to consider what the earl would have done in Peter's place. It wasn't hard to guess what attitude Dunmorrow would have taken, and she turned back to Imelda.

"I thought he might be reading to you," she said in the tone of a mother trying to soothe a frightened child. "He has often read his poems to me, but I fear I have never really understood what they mean. I'm sure you are a far more appreciative audience than I. As for being chaperoned, I have to confess I have just been talking to Sir Percy, and we were quite alone. Please don't disturb yourself. I will only keep Peter a short while, and then I shall send him back to you."

Imelda and Guildford exchanged a horrified look, the latter stumbling out of the summer-house as if his feet had ceased to function.

"Davina," he began, "I can explain ..."

"I haven't time to listen to explanations about your odes now. I want to discuss quite a different matter with you."

"I didn't mean I could explain about my poems, but

about Imelda and I being together."

"Yes, yes. Now, were you by any chance in Ireland at the end of last year; near to Omagh?"

Guildford didn't even hear the question. The moment of truth had been sprung upon him so unexpectedly that he hadn't had time to frame a suitable way to tell Davina of his passion for Lord Russell's daughter. His mind was stuffed full of jumbled words, and feverishly he tried to select one or two which would ease the pain Davina was bound to suffer, no matter how delicate his touch.

"Peter!" Davina was fast losing her patience, and she felt no obligation as far as Guildford was concerned to wrap up her questions. "Did you hear what I said? I asked you whether you were in Ireland last ..."

"Yes, yes!"

He saw the look on her face, wondering what on earth he had said yes to. He had some idea that it was connected with a place which he was supposed to have visited, although precisely where it was had not registered with him at all.

"What were you doing there?"

"There?"

"For goodness sake, pay attention! The question was simple enough, surely? What were you doing there?"

He dared not ask her which place she meant, for she would fly into a rage, and he didn't feel nearly strong enough at that moment to endure one of Davina's tantrums. Hurriedly, he concocted a story which he hoped was convincing and would in some way fit in with whatever she had been asking him about.

"I had gone to see Aunt Agatha. She's very old, and lives so far away that the family can't travel to see her very often, so I ..."

"And that is where she lives?" Davina sounded baffled. "Are you sure?"

The confusion was now so confounded that Guildford was hopelessly trapped in the tangled web of his falsehoods.

The only thing he could do was to go on, and hope that
Davina would soon depart satisfied.

"Yes, I'm quite sure."

He said it firmly and Davina looked more amazed than
ever. She could hardly believe her ears. Had the whole
world been visiting Ireland at the time of the killing, and
was it even remotely possible that Guildford could have
been implicated? She treated him to a long, thoughtful
scrutiny. Peter, who was as fierce as a toothless lap-dog,
and about as pugnacious as a new-born lamb, an assassin?

"Is that all?"

He was perspiring with the strain of the conversation, of
which he had not understood one syllable. She was
regarding him very strangely and a fresh wave of guilt
engulfed him. Of course it was because he had paid hardly
any attention to her since they had come to Ardley,
spending so much time with Imelda. Yet Davina hadn't
complained before, nor made any move to seek his
company.

"Yes," she said at last, "that is all, thank you. Now go
back to Imelda, and don't let her see your hands shaking
like that. You will quite destroy the illusions she has about
you."

She left him with his mouth open and made for the
house, but before she was halfway across the lawn she met
the earl.

All at once she found herself like Imelda Russell, quite
helpless in her love. She wanted to lay her head on
Dunmorrow's shoulder and feel his arms about her, his lips
touching hers.

Promptly she put aside the maudlin longing, very
uncertain of what she should say to Anthony. She was still
fearful that he was the one responsible, yet Sir Percy or
Peter might equally be the culprit. The fact that the
Englishman had fled the country sounded more like Peter
than Dunmorrow, yet Codder and Smythe had been

convincing enough in what they had said, and why should they have lied?

"I cannot imagine what it is that you do to young Guildford which makes him run like a startled buck-rabbit."

The earl's drawl made it immediately obvious that he was going to be unpleasant, and she braced herself to deal with him.

"Peter is not in the least like a rabbit. And what is more to the point, what do you do to Lady Imelda which makes her spend most of her time crying?"

"That is unrequited love."

"For you?" She was waspish. "How very odd!"

"Do you think so?"

He was looking down at her in a way which sapped every bit of strength from her. It wasn't fear which made her legs wobble, and her heart beat at twice its normal pace. She was seized yet again with a wild desire to stroke his cheek, and speak his name softly.

Her day-dream snapped in two when he said nastily:

"Many women have been in love with me; some still are."

"How fortunate for you, my lord! So good for your ego."

"My ego needs no prop."

The well-shaped mouth bore a hateful smile and Davina's earlier wish to stroke his cheek tenderly turned into a positive yearning to slap it very hard.

"And how is yours?" he continued.

"What?"

He was glad that he was not the only one who lost the thread of a discussion. It seemed that Davina was just as bad. Perhaps when they were married, they would be able to concentrate more successfully on what was going on around them.

"Your ego. How is it?"

"Unimpaired," she returned coldly, "even though I

cannot boast of a string of lovers to maintain it."

"I'm very glad to hear it." The smile had disappeared completely. "If you had taken but one, I should ..."

"Yes?"

She knew that she was gaining the upper hand; the earl didn't often break off in mid-sentence.

"I beg your pardon?"

"You were going to tell me what you would do if I had a lover."

Now it was she who was smiling; feline and malicious.

"I will tell you on some other occasion."

"If you have sufficient time left."

The finely-marked brows came together.

"Why shouldn't I have? What are you talking about now? Good God, woman, you are as bad as my father. I've no idea what he means for the most part."

"Then I suggest that you listen more carefully. That should do the trick, unless, of course, you are simple-minded. And, sir, you know quite well what I mean about time running out for you. After what you have done, how could you expect to remain free for much longer?"

He let her go, because he couldn't think what to say next. The purport of her sinister utterance had been quite lost on him, but her eyes were as marvellous as ever, her mouth a deliberate challenge to any red-blooded man.

He wished with all his heart that he could get the Dee business settled. Once that task had been accomplished, he would be able to turn his full attention to the saucy-tongued Davina, forcing her to see the error of her ways after, of course, he had finished kissing her.

* * *

Having talked to Lord Stuart Barminster, and found him as unhelpful and as stupid as Peter and Sir Percy, Davina plucked up her courage and approached the marquis.

She found him in a remote part of the garden, giving

directions to two flunkeys to arrange a dozen bottles on a wall some distance away.

She had considered once or twice whether the earl had been right about his father: certainly some of the things the marquis did led one to suppose he might be slightly unhinged. His present occupation shewed signs of highly erratic behaviour, for on the ground in front of him was a collection of pistols, each a work of art in itself.

"How nice!" His smile was a warm welcome as he waved her nearer. "That's right; just there. No, Jenkins, not on their sides. Stand them up straight as Staple is doing. That's the finest port to be had; treat it with respect."

Davina gasped as one of the precious containers nearly toppled over, her reason for seeking out Ashbourne temporarily forgotten.

"My lord, did you say they were filled with fine port?"

"That's right; the very best."

"But what are you going to do with them, and why are the servants putting them up there?"

"So I can shoot 'em down, m'dear. That's better, Jenkins. Now off you go, and you too, Staple. Here, take this. Buy your wives a trinket or two."

As the two men went off, grinning all over their faces, Davina tried to rationalize the situation.

"Sir, if it is merely shooting practice you need, why don't you use empty bottles."

"Not the same thing at all. Must be full."

"But surely not full of the best port to be had?"

He beamed at her in approbation.

"There now, you appreciate a good vintage, do you? How very unusual, but so lucky for my son."

"Your son?" She watched as the marquis picked up one of the guns and loaded it. "Why is he lucky?"

"I don't really know." Ashbourne paused in his task. "Suppose there was a good fairy at his christening, or maybe he threw a coin in a wishing-well when I wasn't looking. Still, whatever the reason, he's damned fortunate."

He shot her another approving look.

"Very wise of you not to marry Guildford. No style; none at all."

She opened her mouth to inform his lordship that no such decision had been publicly announced so far, when she saw for the first time since they had met the penetrating intelligence in his eyes. It frightened her: was he using that intelligence, and his high position, to help his son escape justice?

Then the marquis went back to his pistol, and Davina threw off the nervous moment. He was nothing but a kind and charming eccentric; quite harmless. Still, charming or not, he mustn't be allowed to make assumptions about her feelings, even if she had admitted to him earlier her doubts about Peter. She said rather coolly:

"Then whom do you suggest I marry?"

He considered the question seriously.

"Well, since I'm rather too old for you, you'd better settle for Dunmorrow."

Side-tracked, and forgetting what the earl might have done, she said even more frostily:

"I doubt if he would want me. And I have to tell you that I am not unaware of your son's reputation. It is said that he has had so many mistresses, he has lost count of them."

"He probably has." The marquis was amused. "One doesn't keep a tally, you know, and, as for his reputation, it pales into insignificance against mine when I was his age."

She remained starchy, for she couldn't bear to think about Anthony's mistresses.

"Not a matter to boast about, surely?"

His smile was tender as he moved closer to her, tilting her chin so that she was forced to look at him.

"Don't confuse what matters with that which is of no importance. Anthony has never been guilty of a dishonourable act in his life, nor has he caused a living soul any lasting hurt."

Ashbourne felt Davina stiffen, sensing the sudden tension

in her. He let his hand fall to his side, wondering what made the girl look as she did. She had been perfectly all right until he had mentioned the fact that Anthony had never harmed anyone.

"Can you tell me what is wrong?" he asked gently. "I'm a good listener."

Davina shuddered visibly. That was exactly what Elliot Dalzell had said on the occasion she had told him she thought the earl might have committed murder.

Ashbourne saw the frisson, and watched her struggle with herself, regretful when she denied that anything was amiss.

"In any event," said Davina rather rapidly, "your son is to marry Imelda Russell, so I can scarcely hope to be his wife."

"That milksop? He'll never marry her. Only offered for her because he was too idle to look for someone he really loved. Also, she's besotted by Guildford. Doubt if she ever looks in Anthony's direction nowadays. Get it sorted out, m'dear. Life's too short to waste precious time, and when you change your mind about whatever is locked up in your heart, come and see me."

"There is nothing in my heart."

Her voice was shaky and he changed the subject at once.

"I'm ready now. Would you like to stay and see the fun?"

Although Davina was remorselessly honest, with no time for polite lies, affectations or fashionable pretences, she had a very sensitive streak in her. Apart from that one rather disturbing moment, she had found Ashbourne the soul of kindness, and it was hard not to grow fond of him.

Since it was improbable that he would be able to shoot even one bottle off the wall from that distance, never mind twelve, she did not want to stay and witness his failure. It would shame him if she saw what the years had done to him.

There was also a more practical reason for her refusal, in that the marquis was quite likely to shoot her in the arm or leg if she didn't get out of the way quickly.

She hurried off, but hadn't gone more than a few steps when the air was split with the sound of rapid fire. She cried aloud, turning in alarm, expecting to find there had been an accident, and that the pile of guns on the grass had exploded in Ashbourne's face.

She felt as though her mouth was full of dust, the same sense of fear besetting her again.

The marquis was down on one knee, holding a pistol in each hand. Every single bottle had been blown to smithereens, the ruby-red liquid running down the stone wall like a tide of blood.

Against her will, she found she was returning to the spot where Ashbourne now stood, as if he were drawing her to him by some inner force. He saw her expression and gave a soft laugh.

"Just practice, and steady hands; nothing more."

She didn't believe him, but of one thing that she was very certain. She had forgotten to ask the marquis where he had been last December, and now she never would.

Whatever else Ashbourne was, he wasn't harmless.

Nine

"Well, Anthony," asked Elliot, "what do we do now?"

Dalzell had been very careful to give no hint of Davina's talk with him, keeping his manner with the earl as easy and friendly as before. It was true that Dunmorrow had many things on his mind at the moment, but any coolness on Dalzell's part would have been noticed.

"I'm damned if I know."

Dunmorrow felt as though he had just come to the end of a blind alley. It would be irksome to have to admit defeat, but there seemed no help for it. At various times of the day and night, he had searched the house itself, whilst Elliot had reported that his excursions into stables and barns were equally unproductive. Both men had ridden out each day, going in different directions, meeting later with a shake of the head, the scouring of the surrounding countryside having been so much waste of time.

The earl reflected again on Blackstone's enigmatic comment: 'Better dead in England, than alive in another place.' He had had no idea what the Regent's Secretary had meant then, and he didn't know now. It was almost as if Sir Christopher had been expecting some such thing to happen, and for the first time the earl stopped to think about Dee's appointment with the prince. 'Always punctilious,' Blackstone had said. So Dee knew the Regent well. Dunmorrow didn't know why that bothered him, but it did. He glanced at Dalzell.

"I can't think of any further action we can take. I had

expected to receive another demand for money, since the man who attacked me didn't get what he had come for."

Anthony hadn't mentioned to Elliot the second man Codder and Smythe had seen: the man who had been expensively clad, and who had ridden away. He had to be careful not to let slip the presence of the two convicts and, if he had gone into great detail, Dalzell might begin to question how he had seen so much, since he had been rendered unconscious.

"Perhaps the man took fright and killed Dee."

"I doubt it." The earl was troubled by the thought. "Dee would be no use to him dead."

"He may not have stopped to think about that if he was in a panic." Elliot was rubbing his chin. "You didn't tell me much about that night, which is natural enough if you had been attacked, but it has always puzzled me why your assailant didn't snatch the money-bag before he ran."

"He may have been disturbed by something." The earl was guarded. "And when I regained my senses, I found I'd fallen on the bag, so he wouldn't have seen it without moving me."

It didn't sound a likely tale, and the earl wasn't surprised to find Elliot eyeing him meditatively. Elliot himself was thoughtful too. He was almost certain that Dunmorrow was holding information back. Anthony wasn't an experienced liar, and it shewed.

"So what will you do?"

"Go to Brighton to-morrow and tell Blackstone that I've failed. What else can I do? Unless between now and then I hear from the kidnapper, I'm helpless. Dee could be anywhere in England by this time.

The prospect of telling Blackstone that he had been of no help made Anthony extremely irritable and, when some two hours later he came upon Davina once more, he wasn't feeling particularly charitable towards the human race.

Neither was Davina. The marquis's suggestion that she

should marry Anthony had made her emotional and on edge. Ashbourne knew there was no possible way in which such a match could be achieved. Lord Russell was a very important man and wouldn't take kindly to Dunmorrow playing fast and loose with his daughter.

Furthermore, Davina had been considerably shaken by the marquis's skill with his guns. The episode had confirmed her belief that he was deranged, for nobody else would have dreamed of wasting good wine, but it proved that there was a great deal more to Ashbourne than one would have guessed at first sight. Mad he might be, but he was quite capable of frustrating the law and getting his son away to safety.

"Ah, madam." Anthony raised his quizzing-glass, a mannerism which was beginning to infuriate Davina. "Lost your beloved one yet again?"

"Not lost, my lord," she retorted with some heat. "I know exactly where he is: he's with your paramour."

The earl gave a thin smile.

"Even if you are losing your temper, you can't seriously believe that Imelda Russell is anyone's paramour."

"Perhaps not. Certainly it would be difficult for her to respond to sexual advances, since she spends most of her time with her nose buried in a handkerchief."

"Not when she's with Guildford. You'll have to watch out for that girl when you're married to young Peter."

"Stop calling him young Peter!"

"Why? He has the mental age of a child of six, and just about as much maturity."

"There is nothing wrong with him." Her ire was rising, for she knew the earl was deliberately baiting her. "He is a kindly person."

"How very exciting."

"My lord."

"My lady!"

"You are the most infuriating, hateful and supercilious

man I have ever met. You don't seem to care about anybody else but yourself and, were it not for your desire to ingratiate yourself with the Regent, you would probably have gone back to London and forgotten the lot of us."

"Forget the Regent? That's easier said than done."

"Oh go away! You are more than I can bear. And as for your father, he is quite insa ..."

"Yes?"

Dunmorrow's voice had grown very chilly and she stopped short. She didn't want to tell the earl about the shooting incident and raised her chin defiantly.

"Never mind. It's of no moment."

"It is to me. You were going to say ...?"

"You said yourself he was mad."

"I said so, but I will not permit anyone else to say it, not even you. Watch your tongue, or you'll be sorry."

"Not sorrier than you. I hope that Imelda makes your life a living hell. You deserve it."

He caught her arm in fingers which felt to her like iron clamps.

"She won't have the opportunity, and neither will you. I shall know how to deal with you when the time comes. Meanwhile, leave my father out of your infantile prating."

"Let me go this instant! You are hurting me, damn you."

"Good, and Imelda never swears."

"But I do and, if you don't release me this very second, I will treat you to a tirade which will make your ears ring."

"And I, in turn, will beat you until your sides smart."

"Oh! You ..."

She managed to wrench herself free and ran. Lying on her bed, her face buried in her pillow, she assured herself most firmly that the earl was cruel and totally impossible, but she could still feel the pressure on her arm. It was marvellous, and they had been so close to one another, their lips only a few inches apart. He could so easily have kissed her, but he hadn't wanted to.

She got up and looked in the mirror, her image blurred

by tears. He was an unspeakable, bullying tyrant, but the world was going to be so dreadfully dull when Anthony St. Romer went out of her life.

* * *

At ten o'clock that night, Davina decided she owed the earl an apology. He had been unbearable, but she had had no right to speak of the marquis as she had, and Anthony had had every right to be annoyed. Much as her own father irritated her at times, she would have defended him with equal vigour.

She looked for Dunmorrow for some time and then asked Rourke if he knew where the earl was to be found.

"Went out, m'lady, about an hour ago. Had an urgent message."

She knew immediately that all was not well. She thought perhaps it was because she loved Anthony so much that some inner sense warned her to make further enquiries.

"Do you know where he went?"

"Well, as a matter of fact, I did happen to glance at the note the man left for his lordship."

"Which man?"

"Didn't see him myself, but Jenkins said he was just ordinary. I asked, you see, because another note was left on the doorstep for the earl a day or two back. Thought it was funny then."

Davina forced herself to remain calm and collected.

"Yes, most strange. Where was the earl to go?"

"Cheshire House. He rode off like the Devil in the wind."

"Cheshire House? Where is that?"

The butler told her and she liked the situation even less. Perhaps that was where Anthony had gone the other night, when she had watched him from her window, and maybe it was in the ruined house that he was holding Christmas Dee.

If he had gone an hour before, there was no time to lose,

and she went to find Dalzell. It was very much like her
search for Anthony; quite fruitless. She was growing more
worried than ever, not sure if she was afraid of what the earl
was doing, or what was being done to him, but she didn't
want the household in an uproar just then. She happened
upon Jenkins, asking quite casually where Sir Elliot was,
only to be told that he had gone out too.

She sat down for five whole minutes trying to convince
herself that the fact that two young men had gone riding at
night was nothing to make a fuss about. But the message
Rourke had spoken of didn't fit in with a pleasure jaunt,
and there was a warning bell ringing in her head.

The marquis didn't answer the tap on his door and this
time it was Alice whom she encountered. When Davina
learned that Ashbourne had also left Ardley, her mind was
made up. She had no idea what kind of trouble was
brewing, but she was quite sure that it was serious.

There was only one thing for it; she would have to go to
Cheshire House too, even if that mean confirmation of her
worst fears. The question was, whom to take with her.

It didn't take her long to decide. Peter, Sir Percy and
Lord Stuart were dismissed out of hand, and she crept
down to the basement, avoiding the servants, making her
way to where Codder and Smythe were hiding.

When she told them what had happened, and mentioned
Cheshire House, Mortimer began to quake and even
Horace was off balance.

"Why do you look like that?" she demanded. "You've
heard of the place before, haven't you? What have you held
back? Tell me immediately, or I shall scream and ..."

"No, no!" Codder groaned inwardly. It was the worst
night's work he and Mortimer had ever done, entering this
house. There hadn't been a minute's peace since they had
first settled there, what with the earl and his threats, and
this chit of a girl, who could be their undoing with one
piercing cry. "Don't ... no ... don't, fer pity's sake. Yer,

we've 'eard of it; we've bin there.''

"You've been to Cheshire House? You mean before you came and hid here at Ardley?''

"No, after that.''

"You left Ardley and went to this place? Why? I was told that it was deserted. What did you want there?''

"It were empty when we was there with the earl ... damn it! Now see what yer've made me do.''

Davina compressed her lips. At last she was beginning to make progress, and her eyes were like daggers on Horace Codder.

"Don't make me drag this out of you word for word; there isn't time. Tell me the whole thing now, or I'll ...''

"I know what yer 'ud do, but for 'eavens sake don't!'' Codder's despair deepened. "I don't know what the earl'll say, but ...''

"Never mind about him. Tell me the truth. What is this all about, and why were you and Dunmorrow at Cheshire House? Is that where you helped him keep Sir Christmas, or his body?''

"Keep 'im!'' Codder saw nothing for it but the real facts. "'Ere, you've got it all wrong. The earl went there to find this man, and we followed without 'im knowin', 'cos we thought it weren't safe. Good thing we did, seein' that 'is lordship was attacked. Could 'ave bin killed, if we 'adn't bin there.''

Davina felt such a flood of relief rush through her that her tongue lost its bite.

"I see, you lied to me. You let me believe that the earl was planning to kill Dee, whereas, in fact, he was trying to save him. Very well, I will say no more about that for the moment. Now tell me the rest.''

When Codder had finished, Davina became very business-like. The load which had been lifted from her mind on hearing that Anthony hadn't harmed Dee was replaced by a fear for his safety. Since he wanted to find Sir

Christmas, he couldn't have been the man about whom
Mirabel's aunt had written. She made her decision quickly.

"You'll have to come with me to Cheshire House."

Smythe began to wail and was reduced to silence by
Horace's fist, but Codder wasn't at all pleased with the
suggestion either.

"We can't do that, miss," he said placatingly. "We
might be seen, and then we'd find ourselves back in
Stockland. 'Sides, there must be others 'ere 'oo could go.
What about a couple of them gentlemen upstairs, or the
servants? Take some of them young lads with you."

"I am taking you," she replied, brooking no argument,
"and, of course, my aunt, for I cannot gallivant about the
countryside at night with two men, unescorted."

"Yer aunt!" Codder didn't believe it. "Fer 'eaven's sake,
miss! She'll give us away."

"No she won't; she'll do as I tell her."

Horace could feel that he was losing the tussle, and she
was right. This hell-cat could make anyone do what she
told them to.

"I have an offer to make to you," she said in a
conciliatory tone. "Neither my aunt nor I will betray you,
and if you come with me I'll give you money, and help you
to get out of the country."

The men's eyes lit up. The prospect was rather pleasing
until Codder had second thoughts.

"Out o' the country? Where'ud we go? Don't want ter go
ter France, nor Spain neither. Boney might get us."

"Go to Ireland," she advised crisply, "everyone else
seems to. Well, what do you say? A handsome sum, and aid
to escape, or shall I ..."

"No! We'll go with yer." Horace got to his feet. It was
certain now that he had been born under a malignant star,
and life was going to lay many crosses upon him. This
termagant was just one more of them. "I'll git a couple of
'orses fer Mortimer and me."

"Yes, and my aunt and I will need a curricle."

"A curricle? What fer?"

"Surely you don't think I'm going to walk, do you, and my aunt will never ride a horse. It's going to be difficult enough getting her there as it is. Get along with you, do! The stables are full of horses and carriages."

"And stable-'ands and grooms." Horace was gloomy. "What we goin' ter do about them?"

"What you always do when someone gets in your way." Davina was making for the door. 'I will meet you outside in twenty minutes."

Twenty minutes was a long time, but Davina judged it would take every second of it to get Rosamond out of bed, dressed, and prepared to accompany her niece to a derelict house, where goodness knows what was going on. She was right. On being told of the plan, Rosamond immediately had the vapours, whilst Horty cried shrilly:

"You can't go out at this time of night, Miss Davina. Whatever are you thinking of? What about the men? The place is crawling with the useless creatures. Send some of them."

"Oh, my head! Horty, a mere drop of brandy, I think."

"Aunt, you don't need brandy. Get dressed."

"I do need brandy, and perhaps more than a drop. Yes, that'll do nicely, Horty. Davina, this is impossible. You can't just go off like this to a deserted house. Who knows what you'll find there."

"I hope to find the Earl of Dunmorrow," replied Davina evenly, "and we are going to take two men."

"That's better, although if the men are going I don't see why we have to. Is Francis one of them?"

"The marquis isn't here. He has gone too."

Rosamond gave another screech.

"Gone? More brandy, Horty. Where has he gone?"

"I don't know, but I suspect to Cheshire House."

"Then who is to accompany us? Not Guildford, I hope,

for he is neither use to man nor beast. Lord Stuart?"

"No, and you'll see who, if ever you put your clothes on and get downstairs. There isn't much time, so do stop clutching your head and drinking spirits. They're not good for you at your time of life."

"Well really!"

Hortensia was forcing Rosamond into a gown rather too tightly fitting.

"He'll get himself killed. He's a fool; a complete fool. I've always said so. Can't even remember my name. Ouch! You're hurting me."

"Shouldn't eat so much, then I could manage without all this tugging and pulling. Fair wears my arms out." Horty was puffing and blowing. "Stand still, will you?"

"You impudent woman, I don't eat too much. I've got an appetite like a bird. It's that wretched dressmaker; she cuts everything too small."

Rosamond turned to Davina.

"You don't think he'll be hurt, do you? Francis, I mean. I pray he won't be, for I don't know what I shall do if he's killed. It will be the death of me too."

Davina was taken aback by Rosamond's anguish. She had been so wrapped up in her love-hate relationship with Dunmorrow, it had never occurred to her that her aunt might also be having trouble with affairs of the heart.

"You and Francis St. Romer?"

"And why not, pray?" Rosamond was very much on her dignity. "I am still attractive, and no age at all."

"Does the marquis feel the same?"

Rosamond turned away, fussing with a shawl.

"I've no idea, I'm sure, but I don't want him harmed."

"No, and I don't want Anthony harmed either, whatever he's done, if he's done anything."

"Anthony? So you've admitted it to yourself at last, have you? About time too. The quicker you send that cretin Guildford packing the better, and what do you mean, if he has done anything?"

Davina evaded the question.

"There's Imelda."

"Stuff and nonsense. Dunmorrow doesn't want her, and I thought you said we had to hurry."

"So we do. Aunt, isn't being in love too dreadful? It's like roasting in hell, don't you think?"

"Only if the one you love doesn't return the feeling, and you needn't worry about that, my dear. Seeing that Ashbourne has been rash enough to go off to this dire place, we'd better follow him, I suppose. Horty, clear the room up; it's a mess. How can you be so untidy?"

They left Hortensia mumbling to herself and made their way quietly out of the side door. Taking all things into account, Davina considered that she had done reasonably well to get her aunt as far as that, but, of course, it wasn't luck. It was because of the marquis.

Her complacency was soon undone when Rosamond caught sight of Codder and Smythe. Davina just managed to get one hand over her aunt's mouth to stop the yell which was quivering on the latter's lips, using her free hand to push Rosamond towards the curricle.

Mortimer and Horace mounted up and Davina took the reins in her small but experienced hands.

"Davina! Who are these ... appalling things? You said two men were coming with us."

"They are men. Your eyes aren't as good as they were."

"There is nothing whatsoever wrong with my eyes, I'll have you know, but these ... these look like ..."

"They have escaped from Stockland Gaol, and I have given a promise that we shall not tell anyone that they are here. I am also going to give them money, and help them to get out of England."

"But why?" Rosamond was turning puce. "Good gracious, have you gone out of your mind? Why are you going to let these wretched specimens escape?"

"Because they may help me to save Anthony's life, and Francis's too, perhaps." She bit her lip. "If only I knew what was really going on, I would know whom to rescue and whom to ... well, we'll see."

Her aunt sank back, temporarily deflated.

"I'm not sure, but I think this matter is very serious. Elliot Dalzell seems to have disappeared as well."

"Mercy! It's that house. First Sir Christmas; then the earl; Francis, and now Sir Elliot. The place must be haunted after all."

"I doubt it." Davina was quickening the pace. "Whatever this is all about it is nothing to do with the supernatural, of that I'm sure. I do think, however, it may be connected in some way with that letter I had from Mirabel."

When her aunt didn't reply, Davina turned her head.

"It was taken from the drawer I put it in. You haven't seen it, have you?"

Rosamond began to prevaricate, but it was obvious to her niece that she knew who had removed it.

"Aunt! Who was it?"

"I promised not to tell anyone."

"You must! It's far too important now to pretend, or to keep promises which you shouldn't have made in the first place. Codder, keep up with us! Don't dawdle back there, or I'll ..."

"Orl right, orl right."

Codder hissed a few choice oaths under his breath. Even hard labour in Australia would be preferable to this.

"Aunt Rosamond, I demand an answer. Who took that letter?"

"Don't be cross with me." Rosamond was almost humble. "Francis assured me that you would be quite safe once he had what he wanted."

Davina felt as though someone was trickling cold water down her spine.

"The marquis? What he wanted?"

"Yes, dear, he wanted Mirabel's note, and I gave it to him."

Davina said nothing more. Why should Ashbourne want the letter, unless it in some way involved his son? But if Anthony was innocent, as Codder and Smythe had insisted so short a time ago, why did he need his father's help?

She glanced back at the two dark shapes following her. She had been too gullible by far. Codder and Smythe probably lied, paid by the earl to concoct the story of an attack, so that he should appear a victim.

She gave her attention to the road again, hopelessly muddled in her thoughts and emotions. Was Anthony guilty or not? It was no good surmising; the only thing to do was to get to Cheshire House as fast as possible where, perhaps, the true answer was to be found.

"There 'tis, miss." Codder's cry broke through her worry. "Over there, on the right. See it?"

"I see it, and do stop shouting. We are not making a cavalry charge; we are going in as quietly as possible."

"Well, at least yer can't scream then, can yer?" Codder gleaned what scraps of comfort he could. "Praise be fer that."

"What did you say? Codder, answer me!"

"It's nothin', miss; nothin' at all. We'll stop 'ere shall we? If we's not goin' ter make a noise, we don't want these 'orses clatterin' about, do we?"

As they drew to a halt, Davina turned to Rosamond again. Her aunt was very subdued for once in her life because she had been caught out in a misdeed.

"Aunt."

"Yes, dear?"

"Do you think the marquis is mad, as everyone says he is?"

"Of course; he's been like it for years. Why do you ask?"

"Because I don't think he's mad at all. I did, until a

moment or two ago when you told me he'd asked for that letter. Now, I think we may find that he's exactly the opposite. Blast them all! What an infernal nuisance men can be!''

Ten

When Davina and her party reached Cheshire House it looked very eerie in the moonlight, and Rosamond began to complain again.

"Hush!" Davina wasn't happy with what lay before them either, but she was made of sterner stuff. "There's a light, Codder. Can you see it?"

Codder took a firmer hold on the stick with which he had armed himself.

"Aye. Reckon we'd do best to turn back."

"Turn back if you want to." Davina was scathing. "Run back to your hole under the ground and hide, and I'll go in by myself."

Horace gave her a black look. There was no way he could avoid entering the place if he were ever to hold up his head again. He pitied the man who found himself husband to this tartar.

"Go on then." He pulled the reluctant and snivelling Symthe after him. "Let's git it over, if we've got ter." He shot Davina another vindictive scowl. "Devil alone knows what we'll find inside. Remember it were yer idea, not mine."

Whatever Davina had expected, and she wasn't at all sure what that was, the reality was an unpleasant surprise. Having groped their way through the open front door, they located the room from whence the light was coming, Davina marching in as fearless as usual.

"Good heavens!"

Elliot Dalzell was leaning idly against the far wall, a pistol pointing at the earl, who was propped up in a corner, his arms tied behind his back, his legs similarly secured. Davina's eyes widened as she saw his face. There was an ugly cut on his temple from which blood was oozing; one eye was closing; there were purple bruises on his cheeks, and his lips were swollen and split.

Rosamond gave one scream and collapsed in a dead faint, Horace and Mortimer trying to draw away as if they wanted nothing to do with what was happening.

Davina's heart sank. So, she had been right after all. Anthony was the man responsible, and Dalzell had proved it, or perhaps even gained a confession. Somehow she had imagined that the earl would be stronger than Elliot, despite the latter's broad frame, and at that precise moment she was more upset by the fact that the man she loved had lost the fight than the fact that he was a murderer. It was typical of Davina's character that she was soon able to brush aside such frailty, nor did she waste time lamenting the extent of Dunmorrow's injuries. Instead, she rounded on Dalzell like a tigress defending her young.

"Sir Elliot, what is the meaning of this? When I asked you for aid, so that I could know for certain whether or not the earl had killed that man in Ireland, and had subsequently murdered Dunn and made away with Sir Christmas, I did not intend you to mistreat him in this barbarous fashion. You should have told me at once that you had established his culpability, and then we could have informed the authorities."

The earl gazed vacantly at Davina. For the first time since Dalzell's men had overpowered him and subjected him to a severe beating, he was afraid. Not for himself, but for the girl who looked as if she were about to claw Elliot's eyes out. He couldn't imagine why she had come, with the now unconscious Rosamond and two nervous convicts.

"Man in Ireland? What man?"

"The one who had so many children that people lost count of them."

Davina could hardly bear to look at Anthony. Whatever he had done, she loved him with all her heart, and the sight of his wounds was making her feel sick.

"It was reprehensible of you to do such a thing."

Dunmorrow found it rather difficult to speak, convinced that his jaw was broken. Beckett, the leader of Dalzell's followers, had enjoyed himself, whilst Jacob and Timothy, his confederates, had pinioned the earl's arms, making it impossible for him to defend himself. Nevertheless, he couldn't just sit there without making some protest against Davina's ramblings.

"If I could understand only one out of every dozen remarks you make, I think I should be content. Please, madam, tell me in simpler words what in God's name you are talking about. I've never laid hands on this fecund gentleman, whoever he was, and why have you come here with your aunt and these two? Don't you realise the peril you are in?"

Davina paused. The earl sounded so convincing that for a second she almost believed him. Furthermore, despite the lack of suitable manpower at Ardley, she was beginning to see that she had been rather unwise to come with another woman, and a pair of spineless criminals.

"Surely, Sir Elliot, you have told his lordship that we are aware of what he has done?"

She hoped that her voice wasn't giving her away. She had to be strong now, for the worst had happened, otherwise Sir Elliot wouldn't have attacked the earl and imprisoned him.

Dalzell spoke for the first time; cool and ironic.

"No, Lady Davina, I haven't, but I feel sure that you are about to do so."

"Yes, I hope you are." Dunmorrow's words were heartfelt. "But don't tell me in riddles. I'm in no mood for them just now."

"Very well."

A decidedly uncomfortable maggot of doubt was beginning to settle itself in Davina's mind. Anthony didn't sound afraid or guilt-ridden, but merely bemused, like one struggling to keep abreast of the tide. On the other hand, she didn't care for the look on Elliot Dalzell's face. For some reason he seemed quite different from the man from whom she had sought help. The deep-set eyes were like stones, the thin mouth quite menacing in its line.

Still, the thing had to be dragged into the open and, in as few words as possible, Davina set out the facts as she saw them, keeping a wary eye on Dalzell's firearm.

The earl felt as if he were taking part in a bad theatrical performance, without knowing either the plot or his lines. When she had finished, her expression more dubious than ever, he said in exasperation:

"You *are* insane! I knew it! It is not enough that my father's brains rattle about his head like dice in a gaming-box. The woman with whom I wish to spend my future also qualifies for a bed in the nearest asylum."

"Don't concern yourself with the future." Dalzell was laconic. "None of you have got one. Your bodies will be found amidst the charred ruins of this house, and I don't suppose anyone will notice that you'd been shot before the flames consumed you."

Davina's lips parted.

"What are you saying?"

"He is explaining to you how we are going to die at the hands of himself and his men outside." Dunmorrow shifted his position slightly, his fingers exploring the knots of the rope binding his wrists. "Don't tell me that you are hard of hearing in addition to everything else. How could you have been so foolish as to walk into this mess? I suppose my only consolation is that your aunt is unconscious, and not shattering our eardrums with her cries."

"She wouldn't do so for long." Dalzell gave a short laugh. "I can't abide hysterical women."

"You!" Davina paid no heed to Dunmorrow or his

strictures. "It was you who took Sir Christmas, not the earl. Where is he?"

"Upstairs, trussed like a chicken."

"Is he still alive?"

"So far. I want information from him, but I haven't had much time in the last day or two to put my questions. After to-night it will be different."

"Information? What could he possibly tell you?"

Davina's hands were clenched at her sides and whatever delusions she had had about Elliot were quite gone.

She had made a dreadful mistake about Anthony, and an even worse one about Dalzell. She couldn't imagine how she could have been so utterly blind, and could have kicked herself for her folly which had resulted in this nightmare. She had had doubts about most of the men at Ardley, particularly the earl, but never once had she considered Sir Elliot, who actually lived in Ireland.

From the very first, she had assumed from the way Mirabel had written that the young Englishman was merely a visitor to Omagh, and it had not occurred to her at all that the man might be permanently resident in that country.

"Who are you? Why have you abducted a gentle old man who wouldn't hurt a fly?"

"Dee is about as gentle as a rattlesnake." For a moment Elliot's cold eyes were amused. "I don't mind you knowing that now, since you'll have no opportunity to talk about it. I was quite perturbed that day, when Anthony told me we were on our way to see Christmas Dee's house, but after a few minutes I began to see the advantages to be gained from the situation. I even persuaded the earl to accept the invitation to stay at Ardley, if you recall. It was a challenge, you see."

"No, I do not see." Davina was short. "I haven't a notion of what you mean."

"A taste of your own medicine," observed Dunmorrow bitterly, "now you know how I feel. Well, Dalzell, why don't you tell us? Don't let us go to our red-hot graves with our curiosity unsatisfied. Apprise us of what this is all about."

"If you wish. Since we have to wait for someone, why not?" Dalzell shrugged. "It's simple enough. My stables make a fair enough profit, but I gamble for rather high stakes, and, alas, have a tendency to lose. I was in considerable debt, with my creditors threatening me, when quite by chance I met a Frenchman. This was some two years or more ago. He made a suggestion of how I could become very wealthy; it was an offer which I couldn't refuse."

Davina by now was too numb to interrupt and Dalzell went on to explain the nature of the offer. He was to become an agent for the Emperor Napoleon, who already paid a number of persons in England to relay to him the state of the nation he so dearly wanted to crush.

But to Dalzell it had been more than a way of meeting his bills. He was by nature an adventurer, thriving on excitement, and balancing on a knife's edge. At first the task had been easy enough. There had been no difficulty in seeing the discontent in England; trade nearly at a standstill; bankruptcies; shortage of food; high prices; government reform postponed. It hadn't been hard either to get information about the naval dockyards, despite the gibbets which awaited anyone caught about the business of espionage.

Then the emperor had wanted more and Dalzell had to find a way to get himself nearer to those in high places. It had meant even less time with his horses than before, but it was worth it. The rewards were very rich indeed.

"Luck was with me." He grimaced. "Dame Fortune had forsaken me at the tables, but she contrived a meeting with the earl, and that was all I needed. He moves in exalted circles and I began to cultivate him again."

"You are an agent for Bonaparte?" Davina found her

tongue at last. "You mean you spy for the French? Sir, you are a rogue. A cowardly, despicable rogue!"

"Not a rogue." The earl was trying once again to slacken the ropes. "Get your facts right for once. This man is a traitor."

Dalzell was unmoved.

"Why not? I like to be on the winning side. England will be forced to sue for peace before long."

"Not without victory." Dunmorrow met Elliot's contemptuous gaze. "You have misread the hearts of those you have betrayed. Your strutting master will be beaten on land as he was beaten at sea. England is stronger than you imagine. She has never given in to the French before; she won't this time."

"Stupid." Dalzell was curt. "You've lived in your world of pomp and privilege for too long, my friend. Ask these two men here, whoever they are, whether they agree with you. They want bread in their bellies, and a coin or two to jingle in their pockets, not empty phrases of patriotism. Gentlemen, what do you say?"

Codder licked his lips. It was a pity he couldn't reach his knife, and Dalzell had gestured to them to throw down their sticks as soon as they had entered the room.

"Well," he said, "it's like this, since yer ask. If it weren't fer that gun, I'd come over there and cut yer throat meself, yer lily-livered swine."

Elliot was white round the mouth, his voice suddenly ragged.

"Be quiet, you scum, or I'll finish you off here and now." He regained his self-control, dismissing Horace and his opinion as of no importance. "Well, it doesn't matter what you think; it never did."

"And you imagine no questions will be asked if I, Lady Davina, Lady Rosamond and Christmas Dee all vanish?" The earl couldn't budge the bonds which tied him: Beckett had done his work too well.

"Doubtless they'll be asked, but I shan't be here to answer them. I shall be in France, or perhaps the Peninsula."

"Since you've agreed to explain things before you roast us," said the earl bleakly, "tell me this. What exactly does Dee do which makes you call him a rattlesnake, and why did you try to take me earlier? I imagine you were behind that fiasco. Why have you abducted me now? If you had left me alone, I doubt if Lady Davina and her aunt would be here, since I presume they are on some sort of rescue mission. You could have saved yourself some bullets."

"They're cheap enough. You really don't know, do you? How remarkable! Blind and ignorant."

"If you say so." Anthony knew it was useless to lose his temper. He could see no way out of their predicament, and he hated Dalzell at that moment more than he had hated anyone before. Not because he was tied hand and foot and aching all over, nor because Elliot thought him a fool and had posed as a friend. His fury, well-concealed, was because Dalzell had got Davina. His beautiful, stubborn, brave and incomparable Davina. "I am blind and ignorant, but that doesn't answer my question."

"Very well, since you are so naïve, I will be more explicit. I didn't think the good marquis would come out into the open to rescue Dee. He and Sir Christmas accept such risks; they are all part of the occupation they follow. When I saw Dee studying me that first day, I knew he would soon realise why my name was familiar to him. I also knew that he'd inform your father that I was here. It was apparent too that Sir Christmas intended to do away with me. That's why he decided to arrange for a number of people to stay with him, including me; he wanted to have me at hand whilst he made his plans. Unfortunately for him, I moved faster than he did. But that wasn't enough for me."

"My father?" Anthony's brows met slowly. "What on earth has he got to do with all this?"

"Everything." Dalzell gave a faint sigh. "I want him, you see."

"But why? I'm beginning to believe you're right. I must be blind or bereft of my wits. What can you possibly want him for?"

"Because he is one of the most dangerous men in England." Dalzell was speaking quietly, as if to himself. "We had never met before he came to Ardley, but I knew all about him, of course. One always has to learn about one's enemies, particularly adversaries of Ashbourne's calibre. I have an enormous admiration for him; such a clever, clever man, with a mind like a devious, twisted labyrinth."

"The marquis?" Davina had been watching Dunmorrow's face, desperately wishing that she hadn't been so naïve herself, first by putting her faith in Dalzell, of all men, and secondly by setting off so ill-equipped to deal with the situation. Now they would all die, and she would never know what it would have been like to kiss Anthony. "Sir, you must be misinformed. He is ..."

She stopped, the remembrance of that brief look which had frightened her coming back with piercing clarity, along with the sight of twelve bottles of best port, splintered into fragments by a marksman of outstanding ability.

"Go on." Dunmorrow was sweating in his efforts to free himself, hoping that Dalzell wouldn't notice the exertion. "In what way is my father dangerous, apart from his proclivity for archery in the dark?"

"Incredible." Dalzell shook his head. "You've lived with him for twenty-five years, and you know nothing about him, do you?"

"I haven't lived with him for twenty-five years; if I had, I would be in a bedlam by now," retorted the earl with unfilial truthfulness. "But since you seem to know him better than I, perhaps you will answer me."

"It will be my pleasure. Even in this benighted country,

the fools who pretend to govern know that there are foreign agents here, just as the emperor realises that there are English spies in France and Spain.''

The corners of his mouth turned down and for a moment his eyes looked as if the sight had gone out of them.

"Where there are spies, there are always spy-catchers. Dee is one of them, but the marquis is the most able of them all. As I said, Ashbourne wouldn't worry about Dee, nor would Dee expect him to. But when your father gets my note, and learns that I have you in my hands, that will be a different matter altogether. For you, Dunmorrow, I think he will come. It will complete my work here most satisfactorily: a jewelled diadem to crown my efforts. Bonaparte will be most generous when I return with Ashbourne as my prisoner.''

"A spy-catcher?'' The earl slumped back against the wall, the breath knocked out of him. It was almost impossible to take in what Dalzell was saying, yet even as he tried to frame words to reject the idea tiny things began to fit together like a kind of mosaic pattern.

They were small flashes of memory: the Regent's manner when he had told him that he was going to buy Christmas Dee's house; Ashbourne's close relationship with the prince and his ministers; Blackstone's assured comment that there was nothing wrong with the marquis's brain-box; an arrow hitting a bull's-eye in a darkened passage; the breaking of his father's journey and his unexpected appearance at Ardley.

"But if you knew who Dee and my father were, why didn't you run?''

"And forego the chance of pitting my wits against the Mad Marquis? No, no, that was the very essence of the thing to me. I would rather have died than miss such an opportunity. As you've seen, I'm rather good at play-acting. I enjoy it. Of course, I couldn't fool Ashbourne as I've fooled all of you, for he knew who I was, but I could play a game of chess with him, with death as the prize. He watched my moves, and I watched his. Now I've trapped him, and I'll take him back to France and force secrets out of him. He won't speak readily, but there is a limit to any man's pain, even the marquis's. No, I would never have run away from that."

Rosamond was coming out of her faint, Davina and Horace helping her to her feet.

"Keep her quiet," ordered Dalzell grimly. "I don't want any noise."

"I thought you intended to shoot us. What do a few screams matter?"

"Shoot us?" Lady Rosamond's bosom heaved. "Davina! What did I tell you? We should never have come here."

"Soon, Dunmorrow, soon." Elliot ignored Rosamond. "Don't be in such a hurry to go to your Maker. Stay and see how I take your father."

"Do you imagine that I won't shout a warning to him?"

"You'll be gagged before long; all of you."

"What ... what is happening?" Rosamond was clinging to Davina, her face the colour of ash. "Why is the earl down there, and what is Sir Elliot doing with that gun?"

"Waiting, Lady Rosamond." Dalzell gave a small, chilling smile. "Waiting for the marquis. He knows I've got Dunmorrow, and he'll be here soon. You won't have to be patient for much longer. It will take him at least another ten to fifteen minutes to reach us, but I think we'd better put the gags on now. I'm sorry, my dear Anthony, that you won't be able to save him, but you see I want him. I want him more than you will ever know."

"And now you have me."

The voice from the doorway was very soft. Dalzell gave a sharp exclamation, turning like lightning, his pistol raised, but he was a fraction of a second too late.

Ashbourne's bullet had gone straight through his body, and Davina, shewing some sign of feminine weakness at last, gave a cry as Elliot collapsed and died in a pool of his own blood.

* * *

"My lord, are you going to tell us the rest of the story?"

Davina, Rosamond and Anthony were in the library at Ardley with the marquis, Sir Christopher Blackstone and Christmas Dee.

"Of course he must." Rosamond had almost recovered from her trip to Cheshire House and was now bristling with righteous anger. She regarded the marquis as wholly responsible for her terrifying experience; it was exactly the sort of prank in which he indulged. "I don't understand half of what went on."

"I think a bit more will have to be said, Blackstone." Asbourne looked across at the Regent's Secretary. "On the understanding, naturally, that they all give their word never to speak of the matter again."

"By all means." Sir Christopher nodded benignly. "And I'm sure we can take their silence for granted. There are a few things I'd like clarified myself, come to that."

"So be it." The marquis smiled at Rosamond. "Although you were ... well ... unaware of what Dalzell said, I imagine your niece has explained most of it."

"Yes, but it didn't make any sense." Lady Rosamond had taken umbrage at the indignities thrust upon her and wasn't going to unbend easily. "Some rubbish about spies and spy-catchers. It's too ludicrous for words. You couldn't possibly catch foreign agents, Ashbourne; you'd never remember their names. The whole thing's a fabrication."

"Do be quiet, aunt." Davina was admonishing. "If you can't bring yourself to recognise truth when you hear it, we can. Please go on, my lord."

"I too heard what Dalzell was saying. I was listening outside the door, which fortunately you hadn't quite closed. He had underestimated my ability to cover distances in a short time."

"Francis! Do you mean to tell me ..."

"Aunt!"

"Oh very well, but I shall have a few words to say to you, my lord, when this is over."

"I'm sorry, Louisa, but I had to wait: I needed to know what Dalzell intended to do. I will continue to call him that, although it isn't his real name. He had adopted many names in his time, but has never used his own: he spared his family that much at least.

"Dalzell had been under surveillance for some time; he wasn't quite as cunning as he thought he was. FitzWarren informed us when he first met that Frenchman, and also when he left for France. He made several trips, and all were noted, as were his stays in London.

"Whilst in his cups, he boasted to Beckett of the way he was outwitting us, but unfortunately a man called O'Farrell overheard him; that's why Elliot killed him. He went back to France immediately, but returned to England at the end of February, when his friends informed him it was safe to do so. No doubt he thought it unwise to go back to Omagh for a while."

"Yet Blackstone suggested that I should ask Dalzell to help me find Dee." The earl gave the Secretary an enquiring look. "Didn't you know who he was?"

Blackstone, who had found time to change his clothes and select another of his apparently inexhaustible collection of vivid waistcoats, chuckled.

"I knew him, but mercifully he wasn't aware of that, so my visit to Ardley didn't worry him. It was a matter of giving him a false sense of security: making him believe that no suspicion fell on him, since he, of all those here, was asked to give you aid. Also, as your father said, we wanted to see what he'd do."

"He and his men damned nearly killed me," replied the earl shortly, "that's what he did, but don't let so small a thing concern you. You were saying, my lord?"

The marquis laughed quietly and went on with his tale.

"Dalzell liked play-acting, as he told you; indeed, he

revelled in it. He thoroughly enjoying adopting the role of Anthony's friend and pretending to look for Dee, whom Beckett and Jacob had hidden away temporarily in the latter's cottage. When I arrived, it was the supreme test for him. Should he leave at once, knowing I'd send men after him if he did, or should he remain and play cat and mouse with me? As you know, he chose the latter for the sheer thrill of it. It was a temptation he couldn't resist."

"I think I would have shot you the minute you came to Ardley," said Davina frankly, "it would have been much safer."

Ashbourne's eyes crinkled with amusement.

"How I envy you, Anthony; what fun your life is going to be! My dear." He looked affectionately at Davina. "He couldn't shoot me in a house full of people. Furthermore, as you know, he wanted to take me alive."

"Why did he want Mirabel's letter? It seemed to be of great importance to him."

"It was. I heard what you said to him about it." Ashbourne was quite shameless. "For once, Davina, you weren't your admirably concise self; the words you used were ambiguous. You implied that Mirabel's note to you was the same as her aunt's to Christmas, but it wasn't, was it? Her aunt's letter mentioned a name; hers to you did not. You spoke of an alias, believing it to be one which Anthony was using to hide his identity. Dalzell knew Anthony was innocent, and was afraid that the name in question was his own. He wanted the letter destroyed."

"But even if he'd torn it up, wouldn't he realise that I'd remember the name, if there'd been one, I mean?"

"Yes, if there had been a name mentioned in your letter, and Dalzell had seen it, of course he would know that you wouldn't forget it. But you would still be working on the assumption that it was an alias which Dunmorrow had adopted, and it would have taken time for you to discover that you were wrong. Elliot had almost finished what he'd come to do; he just wanted to buy a few more days. Without written proof, and Dunmorrow denying your charges, he'd have got the extra time he needed."

"And so you took it from my room to stop him searching it."

"And you. I wasn't sure how far he'd go, particularly if he got it into his mind that it was his true name which was mentioned."

"And did Mirabel's aunt know who he really was?"

It was Dee who answered.

"Yes, she knew him, and his family. It is an honourable one, and his father is a marquis. Sad that he went the way he did. Man like that; ruthless, without fear, shrewd, determined. Would have been worth his weight in gold on the battlefield."

"He was quite wicked." Davina wasn't prepared to consider Dalzell's possible value in war. "Do you know, my lord, I thought at one stage that Sir Percy and Lady Jessica might be involved. I came upon them in the drawing-room one day. They seemed very secretive, and Jessica insisted on Whittingham giving her a letter. I believed it might be Mirabel's."

Rosamond, who had been still for two whole minutes, gave a snort.

"I can tell you what that was. The silly woman had written a love letter to Whittingham, and wanted it back. He wasn't too willing to part with it, for if Jessica had thrown him over he could have made her pay good money for it."

"How on earth do you know that?"

Rosamond favoured her niece with a pitying look.

"She told me, dear; there's no mystery about that. Jessica Barminster never could keep her own countenance."

The marquis went on as Rosamond finished speaking. Elliot's first attempt at kidnapping Anthony had failed because Jacob, sent to do the job, had been disturbed by Codder and Smythe. The demand for money was a blind, and merely intended to make the earl believe the enterprise was one of extortion and nothing more.

"Those two, Horace and Mortimer, told me there was another man there that night." Anthony was looking at his father. "A tall man, handsomely dressed. I suppose there is no chance that you were that second man, my lord?"

"Matter of a fact I was."

"And you left me there?" The earl was incredulous. "Your own son! I could have been dead."

"I made sure you weren't badly hurt. Jacob had gone by then, and I wasn't ready to shew my hand. You were so slow in getting back to Ardley, that I had plenty of time to return here and busy myself with other things."

"The way you ride," said Anthony sourly, "you could have been in Newcastle by the time I got home. Codder's mare had gone lame."

"Quite." The marquis was unmoved by his son's displeasure. "When I first arrived at Ardley, I wasn't sure whether Christmas had gone off to lay plans for Dalzell's removal or not. Then I saw Anthony coming out of his room with a bloodstained handkerchief and realised they'd taken him."

He turned to Christmas, who was busy pouring wine for his guests.

"You're getting slow, d'yer know that? Time was, when Dalzell wouldn't have had time to lift a finger before you'd snapped him up."

Christmas, apart from a cut on his arm and a bruise or two, was as chirpy as ever, his harrowing experience having made no dent upon his ebullience.

"Alas, you're right. Didn't think he'd act as fast as that. Let his man in the side door that night. I put up a fight, of course, but Beckett had a knife, and Dalzell hit me from behind."

"What has happened to Beckett and Sir Elliot's other men?"

Davina saw a veil go down behind the marquis's eyes.

"Only Beckett survived the encounter with Sir Christopher and the soldiers he brought with him. As for Beckett ... well ... he has been most informative."

Davina didn't care to ask any more; she really didn't want to know.

"Did the footman, Robert Gunn, have an accident?" she asked, anxious to get away from the subject of Beckett's fate. "Or did Sir Elliot kill him?"

"Gunn had the misfortune to see Dalzell and Beckett dragging Sir Christmas from his room, so he had to die."

"But Dr Brown said it wasn't foul play."

"Yes, we didn't want to interrupt Dalzell in whatever he was going to do next, so we let him think that he'd pulled the wool over our eyes."

"I take it that you've never met Sir Christmas at Ardley before, since his servants didn't know you."

The marquis patted Davina's hand.

"No, one doesn't you know. Not the thing; bringing such matters into a friend's home."

"Well, I think it's a lot of stuff and nonsense," said Rosamond as they rose and made for the door. "Spies! Utterly ridiculous! It's another of your foolish games, Francis, and it's high time you grew up. They were nothing but a gang of cut-throats, after money."

She swept out as Davina and the marquis exchanged a rueful smile.

"Better she thinks that, m'dear. Don't try to convince her otherwise."

He waited until everyone had gone but the earl. Then he said:

"A word with you, Anthony."

"Of course, but before you begin there's another question I'd like to ask, if it's permitted."

The marquis inclined his head.

"Ask, dear boy; I'll answer you if I can."

"You knew who Dalzell was before you got to Ardley; indeed, it was because Christmas sent word he was here that you came at all."

"True. As you so rightly implied, breaking one's journey from Bath to Cornwall – in Sussex – is hardly practicable."

"Why didn't you arrest him at once? What was it you were waiting for?"

The marquis looked up.

"First I had to establish where Christmas was, and whether he was still alive. Thanks to Blackstone's suggestion that Dalzell should be asked to help you, you sent him out hunting. That gave him the opportunity to check now and then that all was well at the cottage. I followed him."

"Surely he must have known you were doing so."

The pale-blue eyes were serene.

"No, he didn't know. No one ever does. I guessed they weren't ready to kill Christmas, so I could afford some delay. As to why we didn't move at once, we were hoping Dalzell would lead us to the man we really want. Elliot himself was a mere sprat, but he could have pointed the way to the big fish. Unfortunately, it wasn't to be. Never mind; there's always to-morrow."

"Father, I beg you to be careful."

"I always am. How do you suppose I've survived for so long?"

"This man you want." The earl was hesitant. "He knew that he was on delicate ground. "You don't have to tell me if you'd rather not, but is he someone of importance?"

It seemed at first as though the marquis wasn't going to reply, and Anthony was on the point of making his apology when his father said:

"The person in question could not be more highly placed, nor in a better position to do harm."

"You know who he is then?"

"I've always known. The trouble is that I need proof, and if Dalzell had met with him I'd have had that proof. Don't worry, I'll get it before long. It's essential that I do."

Dunmorrow was self-condemning.

"I feel such a complete fool, and so useless."

"There is no need for you to feel either. Dalzell tricked you; he was an expert at it."

"And you, my lord, more expert still." The earl was still trying to come to terms with the fact that Ashbourne wasn't at all what he'd believed him to be. The wild antics, rambling conversations and light-hearted demeanour were no more than a mask to hide a very important servant of the State. Anthony wasn't sure that he liked it. It felt as though he'd met the marquis for the first time that day and was talking to a stranger. There was a painful sense of loss, as if his real father had died. "I was just the bait."

The marquis read Dunmorrow's thoughts with uncanny accuracy.

"Don't look like that. I haven't changed, you know; I'm as I always was. And you were very precious bait to me."

Anthony saw the love in his father's eyes, the magic of Ashbourne's smile working as it always did. He sighed, and the feeling of estrangement melted away as if it had never existed.

"I'm glad, but that doesn't alter the fact that I was gulled, not by one man, but by two. I'd like the chance to redeem myself. Is there nothing I could do to help you?"

The marquis answered obliquely.

"One day, my aim will not be so sure, my reaction not so swift. When that time comes ... Now, what I wanted to tell you was that a day or two ago I sent for Lord Russell."

"Sent for him?" Dunmorrow was fingering a particularly painful contusion on his jaw. "That pompous ass? I thought he heeded no one's summons but the Regent's."

"He came." ,

The earl looked down at his father, and at last managed a wry smile.

"Yes, on reflection, I imagine that most people come when you ask them to. And what had Russell got to do with Dalzell, or whatever his name was?"

"Nothing that I know of. Russell and I didn't meet here, but at some more discreet rendezvous, where I convinced him that he would be wise to accept Peter Guildford as a son-in-law. I think I was rather successful, for in the end he not only thought it a splendid idea, but imagined it was his own. Also, Christmas has decided to go to Scotland after all."

The earl's eyebrows shot up.

"Not because I told him of the rumour, surely?"

"No." The marquis was taking a careful pinch of snuff. "There are other reasons."

"And I'm not to ask what they are?"

"I'd rather you didn't, but the point of my telling you about this is that I've bought Ardley for you and Davina. Plenty of room for my grandsons here. I shall have much to teach them when they start arriving."

The earl was taken aback. In the middle of all that had been going on, his father had succeeded in ridding him of Imelda Russell, and had purchased Ardley into the bargain. Was there no end to the depths of the marquis's talents?

"I don't know what to say."

"I shouldn't waste time saying anything to me. Go and put that poor lachrymose wench out of her misery; Guildford too, of course."

"Yes." Anthony sighed again, this time in relief. "I will, and you have my deepest thanks, sir. Oh, there's one other thing."

"Yes?"

"Those two men; Codder and Smythe. I promised I wouldn't betray them if they helped me, and in a way they did. They were useful when Jacob attacked me, but I've no idea what has happened to them."

"Your enterprising young woman did even better." The

marquis laughed. "She offered them money, and a safe passage from England, if they would go with her to Cheshire House. Don't worry; I've attended to the matter for her. We always pay our debts. Now off you go and ask Davina to marry you. I'm going to try yet again to teach Louisa how to play cards."

"Are you ever going to address her by her right name?"

"Certainly not. She might think I was sane if I did, and that would never do. Go on, my dear Anthony. Davina's waited long enough for you already."

This time, his lordship's smile was a trifle satanic.

"Yes, I'm sure that my grandchildren will love playing with bows and arrows."

"Good God, I hope not," said the earl, and shut the door quickly behind him.

* * *

"So you won't have to marry Guildford after all." The earl had led Davina away from the house, finding a convenient arbour, surrounded by flowering shrubs and trees. It was a remarkably well-planned garden for private assignations. "He and Imelda are at this moment deciding which month they will wed."

"Are they? How touching!" Davina refused to look at the earl. She had thought such terrible things of him that she was really too ashamed to do so, but, on the other hand, he mustn't guess how contrite she was. That would give him the upper hand, a state of affairs to be avoided at all costs. "How do you know that I don't want to marry Peter after all? You haven't asked me how I feel about it."

"It wasn't necessary. I knew already."

She did turn her head at that.

"You are the most conceited ... oh ... your poor face!"

"Never mind about my face; it will heal."

"But it was all my fault. I asked Sir Elliot for help, and told him of my doubts about you. I was so dull-witted that I didn't consider for a second that he might be the man in question, even though the wretched brute lived in Ireland. I am the most stupid woman in the world."

"Magnanimous of you to admit it."

"You have a tongue like an asp."

"And yours is like a cobra's. Do stop wasting time, and tell me that you love me."

"It is for the man to speak first."

She pretended not to notice that he was curling a tendril of her hair round his finger. The look in his eyes was giving her the most unmaidenly thoughts about beds and bedrooms, and she went on rather breathlessly:

"I must say, I didn't imagine my courtship would be at all like this."

"I'll go and pluck a few roses off Dee's bushes if you like," offered the earl helpfully. "I don't suppose he'd miss them, and in any event they'll be ours very soon. What else do you want; a serenade?"

"I want to know how you feel about me."

His finger was now exploring the line of her throat and she shivered, but this time not because of fear.

"Don't be childish. You know how I feel about you."

"Harsh words for one about to ask for my hand, and I assume that that is what you have in mind. Peter didn't insult me when he asked me to marry him."

"He wouldn't have dared, but, if you insist. Davina Temple, I love you. Will you be my wife? Is that all right?"

"No, it isn't! If you can't do better than that, then ... oh!"

Her words were cut off abruptly as Anthony pulled her roughly into his arms and held her close against him. He was just as strong as she had expected him to be; his kiss more satisfying than she had ever dreamed possible.

"God, that hurt!"

"What!" She was startled out of her blissful reverie, her lips beginning to thin. "Are you daring to tell me that kissing me causes you pain?"

"Of course it does, you mettlesome and most beautiful simpleton. Look what Beckett did to my mouth."

"Well, you'll have to put up with it." She was quite heartless. "If you want me to say yes to your proposal, you will have to kiss me again. Dearest, dearest Anthony; just once more?"

* * *

Anthony and Davina found the marquis and Rosamond in the library.

"Very sensible," said the marquis when they informed him of their intention to wed. She's a bit young for me, and I've got my work cut out trying to teach Louisa how to play this simple game. She is being extremely obtuse, and very trying."

Lady Rosamond gave Davina a roguish look.

"Yes, I don't seem to be very good at it, do I? It may take a long time for me to improve. Indeed, it may take the rest of my life."

"You are a schemer, Aunt, do you know that?"

"Of course, my dear, just as you are. You made up your mind to marry the earl the second you set eyes on him. Now confess it."

"Not in front of him; it would make him quite unbearable. He is bad enough as it is."

The earl's hand went round her waist and she sighed in satisfaction.

"We are going for a ride. Is there anything you want?"

"No, my love." Rosamond looked demure. "But be sure to shut the door as you leave; the marquis and I don't want to be disturbed, do we, my lord?"

Ashbourne, who had paid no heed to the conversation, said absent-mindedly:

"No, quite right, quite right. Ah, my trick, I think. That's another thousand you owe me. Louisa, are you sure that you're really paying attention?"

Outside, Anthony's smile was beatific.

"At last I think my prayers have been answered, and I am the luckiest man in the whole world."

For the first time in her life Davina looked shy.

"I'm glad that I've made you happy, and I do love you so very much."

The earl laughed and hugged her.

"That too, of course, yet heaven has showered me with many gifts to-day. I have you, my precious, but I rather think your aunt may have designs on my father, and will soon take him off my hands. Clever he may be, but he's not normal, I swear it. Who else would play bowls in the middle of the night? God help her; I hope she knows what she's doing."

*   *   *

At five o'clock, after tea had been served in the drawing-room, the door suddenly opened and a very nervous housemaid almost fell in.

Dee, who seemed impervious to surprises of any sort, smiled.

"Yes, Maudie, what is it?"

She tried to speak, but her mouth was opening without a single sound emerging, her pallor quite startling.

"What is a housemaid doing in the drawing-room at this hour of the day?" demanded Lady Rosamond. "Where are all the footmen?"

"Yes, an interesting question." Sir Christmas was ruminative. "Where are they, m'dear? Have we mislaid them?"

Maudie managed to answer, not without difficulty.

"They're all outside, sir, that's why Mr Rourke sent me with a message."

"Well, what is it? Don't be afraid; I shan't eat you."

"She's found a dead body!" Rosamond moaned and,

closed her eyes. "That's what it is; it's another corpse in the basement."

"That right, child?" The marquis pricked up his ears at once. "Wasn't here when the first one was discovered. Who is it this time?"

"Francis! Really!"

"He ain't dead, m'lord."

"How very fortunate for him, don't you agree, Christmas?"

"You are quite impossible!" Rosamond was flushed with vexation. "This is no laughing matter. Even if the man is alive, whoever he is, something is very wrong. The girl's shaking like a leaf."

Anthony took the opportunity of kissing Davina on the cheek, since everyone else was looking at Maudie.

"What a wonderful pair they will make!" he whispered in her ear. "My money is on your aunt."

"And mine on your father," she replied promptly. "Hush, Anthony, it may be important."

"So she is; trembling like an aspen." Dee went over to the maid and patted her on the shoulder. "Don't take on so, there's a dear. I won't let anything hurt you. Who is this live body, and why are all the men outside instead of indoors where they belong?"

"That's what I were sent to tells you."

"Well?"

Maudie found it all too much for her and burst into noisy tears.

"Mr Rourke says, please will you come at once, sir," she sobbed, "soon as you can. Is 'ighness, the Prince Regent, 'as just arrived."